One Deadly Take

D.B. BORTON

The Cat Caliban Mysteries Book 1

JOFFE BOOKS

Revised edition 2025
Joffe Books, London
www.joffebooks.com

First published in the USA in 1993 as *One for the Money*

This paperback edition was first published
in Great Britain in 2025

Cover art by Dee Dee Book Covers

ISBN: 978-1-83526-935-0

A NOTE TO THE READER

Please note these books are from the 1990s, a time before DNA testing and CCTV, when social attitudes were very different and smartphones were not ubiquitous.

To Casey in loving memory of eighteen years of co-authorship

CHAPTER 1

"You don't look like no 'tectives on TV, Granny," Ben had announced at his first opportunity to comment on my new career. He'd stuck one pudgy digit up his nose and pointed another one at me accusingly. "None o' them gots white hair."

"Stick around for a few seasons, kid. They will," I'd answered.

What the hell. I was used to skepticism. Any veteran mother that isn't has her goddamned ears stuffed with kumquats.

Swearing was a habit I'd picked up when Fred was alive. One day I got the impression that Fred hadn't been listening to me for a while. Say, twenty years. So I thought I'd try a little verbal variety to see if he'd notice. At first, it was just an experiment. Then, you know, it became a challenge; tomorrow he'll notice, I'd think. There toward the end, though, I didn't want him to break his record. But I didn't cheat. And Fred Caliban went to his grave believing I was the same sweet girl he'd married. Since I'd never actually been sweet, either, except in Fred's imagination, you can see how alert he was.

It's no wonder I'd wanted a change when Fred died. See, I had this epiphany in the women's john at McAlpin's Department store in downtown Cincinnati. But that's another story — maybe I'll tell you when I know you better. What I wanted was THE change, but I figured I'd better make my own change, since Mother Nature, like most mothers I know, was overextended and running behind.

I loved my kids as much as the next mother, but three kids and thirty-eight years of marriage didn't seem like much to show for more than half a century. Oh, the kids came out okay, I guess, even though now that they were grown up and could tell me what to do they could be regular pains in the ass. Sharon was a successful stockbroker who had negotiated a merger with a male stockbroker as practical as she was, and they had produced one child, Benjamin, the hair color critic. As the oldest of my offspring, Sharon claimed the privileges of seniority when it came to giving me advice. My second child, Jason, was some kind of business executive on his third marriage and his fourth kid. You might've thought his own mistakes disqualified him from telling other people what to do, but he was Sharon's ally. Then there was Franny, my favorite, who was off somewhere attending school. I lost track the fourth time she switched colleges and majors. She was the original boomerang kid: she always came home to her mother when she couldn't think of anything else to do. The myth of the eternal return, which Franny had tried to explain to me when she was an anthropology major at Michigan, was no myth as far as I was concerned.

Then there was my better half, Fred, as dull and familiar as the Council on Dental Therapeutics statement on the Crest toothpaste tube. My generation of women didn't think much about divorce once the initial postwar flurry died down. We didn't expect marriage to be different with anybody else short of Rock Hudson, who was even less available than we knew. It never occurred to us to live on our own. With what? Besides, the women's magazines were crammed with advertisements featuring lonely spinsters of thirty whose lives had been ruined because of halitosis or body odor; we were supposed to be lucky.

So with Fred gone I'd wanted a big change, and I'm not talking facelift and hair color. I wanted a new career. I'd read those articles about looking at your housekeeping skills from the perspective of work experience — accounting, management, personnel supervision, maintenance. I reassessed all my skills and surveyed the reading I'd been doing for the past twenty years. That's how I came up with the idea of Cat Caliban Investigations, a private inquiry agency.

Hell, I'd investigated things all my adult life. Who left the freezer door open so all the ice cream melted. Who left their new purple T-shirt in the washer so that everybody's underwear turned lavender. Who drew stripes on the cat with Marks-a-Lot. Why couldn't Fred ever think of anything to give me for my birthday.

Besides, it was the 1980s, for chrissakes; women were doing all kinds of jobs.

Not that I expected to be an overnight success in the private investigation business. I figured on a training period and anticipated a cash flow problem. I'd talked it over with my friend Louella, who had taken up real estate after her husband, Art, died. Louella had found me a little apartment complex to buy, four units in pink brick, a square little box of a building with an add-on office, a greenish-brown lawn, and two medium-sized spruce trees to match. Good rental history. Solid investment. I threw a yard sale at my three-story house in Wyoming — a neighborhood full of nuclear families, middle managers, and Suburbans — packed up the leftovers, and moved to Northside. Carved over the doorway in white limestone was somebody's idea of a classy name: The Patagonia Arms. Needless to say, after I moved in, it became known among my friends as the Catatonia Arms.

About a week after the move, I'd been shampooing a layer of cigarette smoke and beer off the forest-green wall-to-wall in the living room when I'd caught a glimpse of Herb Munch, Fred's best pal, standing out front. He was shaking his head over the signs — the one for the Patagonia Arms, and the one in the yard for the two vacant apartments. Herb looks like a tall Jack Nicholson with glasses and all the angles and edges blunted, but he doesn't have Jack's stature. Sophie and Sadie were perched on the windowsill like bookends, glaring at old Herb, their tails whipping back and forth like streamers in a snow squall. They'd never liked Herb, either. He had the bad manners to ignore them. I hoped their little brother, Sidney, was lurking by the front door playing attack cat. I had never agreed with Herb Munch about anything, from the pennant race to Fred's fucking funeral arrangements.

A yelp of pain announced that I had been right about Sidney; when I opened the door, he was stuck to Herb's ankle like a little black burr to a coyote's coat. He had his teeth sunk into Herb's argyle socks.

"Why, Herbert! What a pleasant surprise!"

"Get him off me!" Herb bellowed, hopping on one leg and waving the other. Sidney was flapping around like a flagpole sitter in a high wind, but he was damned if he was going to let go.

"You don't have to shout. My goodness! He's only doing his job." I detached Sidney, claw by claw, from Herb's pant leg, and bussed him on the nose. "Good kitty! Good boy! Next week Mother will explain the difference between bill collectors, Mormon missionaries, and friendly visitors." This was for Herb's benefit; I didn't consider him a friendly visitor, and we all knew it. "You see, Herb, he needs encouragement."

"He needs drowning," Herb muttered. He stalked past me, flung himself into a chair, and rubbed his ankle.

"Do come in, Herb, and make yourself comfortable."

"You didn't even tell me you were moving." He sulked. "I heard it from Dave up at the bank."

Men can never take a hint, have you noticed? Now if a woman discovers that someone has moved and sent change-of-address cards to everybody from the dry cleaners to *TV Guide*, does she come around and accuse that person of oversight? Subtlety and perceptiveness are secondary sex characteristics, take it from me.

"That so," I said. Noncommittal.

"When did you decide to do all this, anyway? And who did you talk to about it?" Translation: why didn't you talk to me? "I'm worried about you, Catherine. You just don't have the experience to manage real estate, and as for a detective agency—" He gestured vaguely, as if it were hardly worth discussing, which it wasn't. He spoke sadly, as if he were giving me bad news that wouldn't have occurred to me.

"I talked to Louella Simmons about the real estate, to the reference librarian and the ghost of Dame Agatha about the career change, and to the cats about both. You're the first wet blanket. Do me a favor, Herb. Don't worry about me."

"Louella Simmons doesn't know shit about real estate, excuse my French."

"Your fucking French is excused. Louella has a realtor's license and a gold jacket."

"Hell, any flea-brained housewife can get those things, Cat."

I tried withering him with a look since I hadn't started my karate lessons yet.

"And where did you get the idea that you could be a detective? Have you been taking a correspondence course? Private investigation takes years of training. Can you fire a gun? Can you pick a lock?"

"Nancy Drew had less training than I have. I've been reading detective novels for years. I can pick up the skills I don't have."

"Oh, yeah, when? When you're looking down the barrel of a gun?"

Herb was beginning to get on my nerves. He prided himself on his sense of the dramatic.

"I don't understand you, Catherine. Fred left you well off. Not rich, maybe, but well off. At your age, you should be relaxing, taking life easy."

"If I took life any damn easier than I have the last ten years, I'd be dead, for chrissake. You don't understand me,

Herb. Fine. I don't expect you to. I like it that way. The day you understand me, I'll shoot myself. Now, why don't you just go away, and let me get on with my goddamn life."

I was already restraining Sidney, who sensed the opportunity for a reprise in the air.

"Fred must be turning over in his grave," was Herb's parting shot.

I doubted it. If Fred turned over in his grave, it would be to say, "What was that, Cat? Did you say something?"

Sadie, my pepper-and-salt tabby, had the last word. She strolled to the door, turned her back on it, dug her claws in the carpet, and buried the departed Herb like a turd in a litter box. The curse of kitty disdain.

Who the hell was Herb Munch to tell me how to run my life? My own kids were bad enough. Whatever possessed me, they wanted to know, to buy rental property in Northside, a working-class neighborhood known for its condemned houses and Goodwill store? Property values hadn't increased there since the great Dutch elm disease plague. The only people who were willing to move into the neighborhood and fix up their houses were yuppie lesbians, and even they were buying on the Urban Homesteading plan. Surely I wasn't planning to live there! Four blocks from the army-navy surplus store and the second-hand refrigerator store, and five blocks from Park's Chili? And I was planning to start a *what*? What did I know about detective work? Did I realize how dangerous it was? I would probably get blown away on my first case.

"Fine," I'd said. "Then you can contest my will on the basis of insanity."

Franny, as usual, was the exception.

"I think it's a gas, Mom," she'd said on the phone, calling collect from Albuquerque. "I'll trade in the monogrammed hankies I bought for a semi-automatic for your birthday."

"That's okay, Fran. Detectives still use hankies — you know, to pick up murder weapons without smudging the fingerprints." I knew the kinds of places Franny shopped. When the kids were growing up, I'd found a use for all their presents so that I wouldn't hurt their feelings. But a handprint ashtray was one thing; a deep-discounted Saturday night special was another. Some sacrifices I was not prepared to make.

And another thing, why does everybody make such an issue of my age? I'm young for a detective. Look at Jane Marple. Look at Maude Silver. Look at Mrs. Pollifax, for chrissakes.

I stand five-feet-one in my Adidas, but nobody would ever mistake me for Miss Petite America. Eating is one of the pleasures of life, in my book, and it was one of the few pleasures available to me when Fred was alive. I conceded, however, that Mrs. Pollifax made a more appropriate role model for me than some of the rest — hence the prospective karate lessons.

Meanwhile, I'd already gone out and bought a working girl's wardrobe, with dark color pantsuits like V.I. Warshawski wears. Standing in the dressing room at Shillito's, I shrugged my shoulders up and down and swung my arms around to make sure there was enough room for a shoulder holster in case I ever learned how to use a gun. There would be, as soon as I dropped ten pounds at the Y. I drew the line at silk blouses, though; they seemed so impractical. V.I. was always getting hers bloodied up and ripped to shreds, and at thirty-five bucks apiece I couldn't see the point. Maybe cheapness was an attitude that came with raising three kids.

Kevin, my tenant, agreed to take shooting lessons with me. My friend Mabel had been worried about this facet of my new career. To tell the truth, it worried me a little, too.

"The only weapon you know how to shoot is your mouth, Cat. How you going to be a detective if you don't know anything about guns?"

"Miss Marple never fired a shot," I'd said.

"Yeah, but this is no rural English town out of the 1930s. This is the eighties. The twenty-first century is just around the corner. Plus, this is the city, like they say on TV. And on TV *these* days, the guy without the gun gets wasted."

So I'd told her about the lessons.

"You're taking shooting lessons with a fairy?"

Sometimes I swear I thought Mabel's consciousness hadn't budged since 1951. It was like the sixties had happened in somebody else's lifetime, not hers. I'd been trying to reprogram her for seven years, but it was an uphill battle. She'd spent too many hours bending over a steam iron, and it had affected her gray matter.

"What does his sexual orientation have to do with it? I want to take a class with him, not go to bed with him."

This was too deep for Mabel.

Kevin O'Neill had come with the apartment building when I bought it. He was Louella's pièce de resistance: a quiet tenant with a steady job as a bartender, a man who always paid his rent on time.

"And," she'd enthused, "he's a fabulous cook!"

He'd seemed nice enough when I met him. Average height, slender, reddish-blonde wavy hair, a faint sprinkling of freckles, and smoky blue eyes. But the cats, little emotional beggars that they are, got to know him before I did.

On a sweltering Saturday in late July, I'd puddled out to the sidewalk to call the cats. I hadn't seen them for hours, and I thought it was time to check for dehydration. Kevin stuck his head out of the door at Number 2 — across from my apartment on the ground floor.

"They're in here, Mrs. C. Why don't you join us? I popped some banana bread in the oven a while back, and it'll be done any second."

"The oven?" I echoed, aghast. My oven hadn't seen service since I'd tested it on a tour of the property. Who ate hot food in a heat wave? I went in and stood dripping all over his Persian rug. The apartment smelled like bananas.

Cats have that famous sixth sense. It tells them that someone is going to come to the door half an hour before the bell rings. It tells them which is your last pair of run-less pantyhose. It warns them, from a distance of fifty feet, when their dinner has been doctored with medication or vitamins. And on hot days it locates the only apartment in the neighborhood with air conditioning. Survival of the fittest. Kevin's window units were working overtime and his apartment felt like a meat locker after the tropical air outside. The cats were sacked out on the sofa, watching the Reds get pounded by the Astros. Nevertheless, they looked totally blissed out, as Franny would say. But totally.

"I can't stay. I just wanted to check on them. They look okay to me, as long as you're willing to vouch for the fact that they're still breathing."

The Landlord's Handbook, which I'd picked up at B. Dalton's the week I decided to become a real estate mogul, had devoted a whole chapter to landlord-tenant relations. It warned of the dire consequences of intimacy — or even friendliness — between landlord and tenant. It admonished novice landlords to maintain tenant relations on a strictly business level. Breaking banana bread with your tenants was, I suspected, off limits.

"Oh, come on, Mrs. C," he said, bustling into the room with a tray of banana bread and two Cokes. "Pull up a chair and cool off. If you don't help me out, I'll be forced to eat the whole loaf myself and spend the next two weeks exercising to get rid of it."

I had not read *The Landlord's Handbook* to the cats. As soon as Kevin sat down on the couch, Sidney climbed into his lap, purring like a jackhammer, and Sophie snuggled up against his thigh. Sadie was too far gone to notice. With a sense of crossing the Rubicon, I sat down.

During the seventh inning stretch, we discussed my plans for Caliban Investigations. By now we were Kev and Cat, Cat and Kev.

I showed him my copy of the Ohio law covering licensure of private investigators.

"The 'good reputation for integrity' shit I can fake and I haven't been convicted of a felony or moral turpitude in the last twenty years. So the only problem I see is with the part about two years of experience in 'investigatory work for a law enforcement or other public agency, et cetera.' What the hell am I going to do about that?"

"I wouldn't worry about that," he said. "I'm sure you can always buy your way in in a pinch."

"Do you really think so?"

"Sure. How do you think this state operates anyway?"

Two hours later, I left with Kevin's promise to take shooting lessons with me.

"I look on it as acquiring another job skill, Mrs. C." He shrugged, reverting to his preferred form of address.

So as far as *my* job skills went, I'd covered some of them by signing up for lessons. As for the rest, hell, I had a library card.

CHAPTER 2

"*READING IS THE KEY THAT UNLOCKS EVERY DOOR.*"

I looked at that poster every damn day in second grade. Skinny little white girl with Shirley Temple curls and a pinafore, and a little white boy with a butch haircut and a mouth like a zero, hands in the air, standing in front of this heavy wooden door like something out of *The Seven Voyages of Sinbad.* The door was partway open, with rays of light shooting out, and you could see things behind the door — pirates and bears and fairies and knights and princesses and doctors. It made a hell of an impression on me and I took its message to heart.

So what I did was I made up a list of everything I needed to know about in order to be a detective: forensic psychology, law, ballistics, handwriting analysis, toxicology, accounting, and all the rest. Then I ranked my topics in order of importance. I figured it was more important to know how a gun worked, for example, than how to recognize indigenous plant and animal poisons of North America. And what caused rigor mortis and how long it lasted was more important information, at least in the beginning, than the psycho-sexual roots of multiple personality. But accounting was up there near the top of the list. A business is a business.

Then I took my list down to the public library and threw myself on the mercy of the reference librarians. Four days a week now for the past two weeks I'd staked out a table in the library and read. Me and the other regulars — the winos and street people — were on the verge of becoming chummy. I read about rigor mortis, and they demonstrated it. I'd already learned something about Ohio inheritance laws. About wire-tapping and common types of industrial espionage. About bullet wounds, entry and exit holes, types of bullets.

On Wednesdays, I drove around the city. I figured I should familiarize myself with the neighborhoods — not just the ones where the kids had played soccer, baseball, and tuba, but all the neighborhoods. Over-the-Rhine, where tenements stood shoulder to shoulder with gentrified townhouses. The West End, which looked like a war zone after everybody'd gone home. Western Hills, a bastion of Appalachian insularity. Roselawn, home of the Hot Bagels shop and kosher delis. Yuppied-up Hyde Park. Artsy-fartsy Mt. Adams. Sometimes I practiced tailing people — on foot or in the car.

On Sundays I practiced miscellaneous skills. I tied and untied knots I learned out of an old *Boy Scout Handbook* I found around the house. I wired and rewired plugs and outlets using Jason's junior electrician manual. You can never tell when a skill like that will come in handy. The cats lay low, so nobody got hurt when my first plug exploded, shot across the room like a guided missile, and defoliated the lower branches of my Norfolk pine. "Practice makes perfect" is my motto. Next month, I was planning to work on hot-wiring cars. I was still looking for volunteers.

Then there was the junior chemistry set, although so far, I didn't think I'd learned much that was useful. I'd learned how to mix up something that foamed like draft beer. I'd learned how to make a weather dog whose eyes turned pink or blue depending on whether it was going to rain or not. And I'd learned how to make a rotten-egg smell without using rotten eggs. You see what I mean? Clever, but how practical? I could clear a room in five minutes as long as I was willing to tote a Bunsen burner around with me. I was enjoying the results of this last experiment when two prospective tenants showed up. I'd already caught a glimpse of the three cats disappearing in the direction of Kevin's, noses quivering, dragging their little overnight cases.

Melanie Carter, the quieter of the two, was tall and impressed me as being powerfully built for a woman. Shoulder-length curly brownish-blonde hair, sleepy brown eyes, thin lips. She wore a pair of wrinkled pants and a short-sleeve shirt and the unhappy look of someone who's been required to dress respectably. Alice Rosenberg, who did all the talking, had short thick black hair, bluntly cut and left to its own devices, and gray eyes. She wore a sensible skirt and blouse as if they were a second skin, and, more sensibly still, no hose. She was trying to ignore the odor. Melanie was holding her nose. I decided to show them the apartment over Kevin's.

Alice Rosenberg and I traded chitchat on the stairs — not the kind running to self-disclosure. I figured they were a couple, but I didn't ask. None of my business. Who knows what they thought I was. I slipped the key in the lock, turned it, and pushed the door open. I got two steps into the room and froze. They bumped into me like railroad cars.

In the middle of the floor a woman was lying face-down. The room had a smell even stranger than rotten eggs, and there was a dark stain on the carpet where the woman was lying. Melanie spoke for the first time, her voice deep and husky.

"I don't think your last tenant has vacated, Mrs. Caliban."

There was nothing in the goddamn *Landlord's Handbook* about this.

CHAPTER 3

I was upstairs talking to the cops. Sergeant Fricke, who looked like he'd passed the last police fitness exam by bribery, wanted to know whether I'd moved the body and all. I told him that I'd felt her neck for a pulse and started to turn her over, but when I saw the knife in her chest, I left her alone. I was afraid I was going to lose my lunch all over the damn carpet, if you want to know the truth, but I didn't tell him that.

The woman was elderly, with a weathered face something like crushed aluminum foil. She was on the small side, and she was overdressed for August. Her wispy white hair was covered by a knit cap, and everything she wore she wore at least two of. The reason I noticed was that everything was unbuttoned and unzipped, as if someone had searched her after she was dead. It had to be after, because there were pieces of cloth stuck to the knife. The clothes themselves were wrinkled and patched and not too clean. Nothing matched. She looked like a bag lady to me, except there was no bag — only a bus transfer, which I'd spotted on the carpet nearby and left for the cops to find.

The sergeant asked all those stupid questions cops have to ask. Did I know who she was? Did I know what she was doing in this apartment? Was I sure the door was locked when

I found her? Had I shown the apartment to anybody else? Who lived below? How long had he lived here? How long had I lived here? Had I seen or heard anything unusual in the past few days?

It had already occurred to me that she'd been here a while. But I hadn't boned up on rigor mortis for nothing, and she didn't have it. On the other hand, if she'd been here much longer, the cats would have caught on. That they hadn't sniffed her out already suggested to me that their senses were numbed by too much air conditioning — especially since now that I'd gotten a snootful myself, I couldn't believe that I hadn't smelled something. I supposed that between Kevin's baking and my experiments, the olfactory battle being waged inside the Catatonia Arms was enough to mask the odor. By now I was feeling more sick at heart than sick. To think that she'd been lying up there, maybe a day or more, and I hadn't known. Had she needed a place to sleep and found an empty apartment? How had she gotten in? Who had killed her, and why? Why here? She had certainly been murdered. Somebody had searched her, I was pretty convinced of that, and somebody had locked the door afterward. It gave me the willies — me, Cat Caliban, Private Investigator.

At one point I remembered that in mystery novels the person who finds the body often ends up getting arrested for murder, and I began to worry about the felony conviction clause in the state licensure law covering private investigation.

Kevin was in his element. He treated me like an ailing grandmother, ushering me into the kitchen and plying me with tea and poppyseed cake. To my surprise, Melanie and Alice were sitting at the table. They looked a mite pale.

Kevin went off to talk to the police after securing my promise to post bail if anything should go wrong. I apologized to Melanie and Alice for the way their day had turned out, and Alice said it was okay and could they see the other apartment sometime? I put this down to politeness and said if it was all right with the police, it was all right with me. After a minute I added that I was not aware of an especially high crime rate in this building. I'd been there three weeks already, and this was the first murder we'd had.

Kevin returned to make coffee for the cops — French roast. Melanie and Alice went upstairs to talk to the cops, the cops came downstairs to talk to all of us together, Sidney made an entrance attached to Sergeant Fricke's pant leg, and somewhere in there an ambulance arrived and took away the body.

When everybody left, Kevin sat down and said, with a conspiratorial air, "Well? What do you think?"

"I don't know what to think," I said. "Why would somebody murder somebody in my upstairs apartment?"

"Not about that. About the girls."

"Melanie and Alice? We'll never see *them* again."

"The tall one is a martial arts expert and an artist. The short one is an attorney with Legal Aid. They like women's music and jazz. They're perfect for us!"

Kevin collected information the way flypaper collects flies.

"Yeah, well, I hate to spit on the bonfire of your enthusiasm, but would *you* move into a building where somebody'd just been murdered? I take that back. How many people do you think would move into a building where somebody's just been murdered?"

"Well, they know we're not boring."

"Sure, but do they know we're safe?"

"Hey, listen, if I was a martial arts expert, I might look on it as a challenge. How often do you think she gets a chance to use her skills?"

"Look, if she really wanted to use her skills, we're small potatoes. She could move downtown and mix it up with the drug traffickers and the youth gangs."

"You think we don't have drug traffickers in Northside?" I could see Kevin's neighborhood pride was aroused.

"I don't think I want to know about it. The point is—"

"The point is you're running a business here, Mrs. C. You just had two live ones walk through the door, no offense to the recently deceased, and you're not going to close the deal because of a measly murder on the premises. You've still got one apartment vacant—"

"Oh, God, I hope so!"

"—one apartment vacant, without so much as a breath of scandal to blot its reputation—"

I winced at Kevin's tendency to mix unfortunate metaphors in the heat of argument.

"—not a single stain on its character, plus reasonable rent, prime location, charming management, fascinating neighbors—"

"Off-the-street parking, paid heat, and a dead body across the hall."

"Are you a businessman or a mouse?"

"Definitely a mouse. A businessmouse."

"No, you're not. You're a real estate entrepreneur and a private investigator. You've now got a murder to solve and two empty apartments to fill. What more do you want? Anyway, what do you think will happen when Fred's old pal, Howard Mooch—"

"Munch. Herb Munch."

"—Herb Munch gets wind of this and comes to see how your new ventures are prospering?"

"If he says 'I told you so,' I will murder him with a blunt instrument."

"In which case you'll need an attorney from Legal Aid. Why not rent her the apartment and save the hassle of parking downtown?"

He had a point. It had not escaped me, as I said before, that Kevin and I were prime suspects in the murder upstairs and stood to be arrested any minute.

"Why would somebody pick this building to murder somebody? And why this poor woman—"

"Betty Bags."

I stared at him.

"Don't give me that withering look, Mrs. C. I didn't make it up. That's her name."

"How do you know?"

Kevin waved this aside. How did he know anything? He was probably the only civilian in the country who had known about the Watergate break-in before Nixon. What he didn't know about the Kennedy clan wasn't worth discussing.

"So she *was* a bag lady, or is it a 'street person'?"

"Under the circumstances, I think 'bag lady' would be the most apropos."

"I see what you mean. If she was a bag lady, where were her bags?"

"I just *know* that you're going to succeed at this detective racket, Mrs. C! You have such a penetrating mind!"

"Okay, cut the sarcasm, if you don't mind! One minute, you're all staunch support, and the next, you're trashing my acumen. Shit, if Nancy Drew had you to contend with instead of just Hannah Gruen, she never would have made it as far as the golden pavilion."

"Sorry. I'll be supportive. What's your plan?"

"Well, I guess I should see what the police come up with first."

"Right. No challenge to a case if the cops can solve it."

"And if nothing happens, I'll try to find her friends."

"Alice's friends?"

"No, you asshole. *Betty's* friends. Street people."

"Oh, *Betty's* friends. Do you think that might be dangerous?"

"Only if one of them clobbers me with her shopping bag."

CHAPTER 4

That was Sunday evening. On Tuesday, a pair of bodybuilders in muscle tees showed up, introduced themselves as friends of Kevin's, and cleaned the upstairs apartment. They ripped up the living room carpet, made it disappear, and left behind a gleaming wood floor that smelled of wax. The following Sunday, to my amazement, Alice Rosenberg and Melanie Carter moved into Number 4 — the apartment with no history as a scene of the crime. The thermometer registered ninety, and my watchcat lay limp on the front stoop like a little black welcome mat. Melanie appeared with a complete stereo sound system balanced on her shoulders, and stepped over Sidney. Alice brought up the rear, lugging a speaker. I spotted one blue eye in a crack at Kevin's door, then it vanished and the door closed silently but firmly. Kevin was good-natured and had a flair for self-dramatization, but he didn't aspire to martyrdom. I stood in my doorway trying to look my age and smiled encouragement.

We shouldn't have worried, as it turned out. My two tenants were assisted by an army of amazons who toted bookcases, dressers, and a couch as if they were gigantic boxes of spaghetti. These girls had muscles. Even Sidney moved out of their way when he saw them carrying the barbells.

Kevin's door opened and he watched the weights ascend. "I feel safer already," he said. "No more murders in *this* building." He retreated and the door closed.

Sophie and Sadie were nowhere in sight. I assumed they were cowering in Kevin's air-conditioned sanctuary, along with Kevin. If I knew Kevin, and I was beginning to feel like I knew him well, he would emerge with a plate of cookies just as the last box disappeared up the stairs. The melodious strains of a woman folk singer's voice were already issuing from Number 4. I went back into my apartment and practiced breaking into Fred's desk.

It was too damned hot to concentrate, and there wasn't anything in Fred's desk worth breaking into it for. *Just once,* I thought, *if just once he'd surprise me.* A packet of steamy letters in a secret drawer. A pornographic novel underneath a false bottom. A later will in a hollowed-out leg, leaving his beige Pinto to his illegitimate daughter. A birthday list for me that had something on it I wanted. Anything. Upstairs, women were laughing, chattering, and heaving furniture around. I bet they were having fun.

The cookies appeared half an hour later and Kevin prevailed upon me to help deliver them. I told him he should take Sidney if he felt the need for male support, but he said Sidney had joined the women an hour ago. Sure enough, when we walked in, Sidney popped out of an empty box and ambushed us. A tall, tanned woman with a long black braid pounced on him and tickled his stomach as if they were old playmates. He squirmed with delight.

Alice emerged with a vacuum cleaner hose wrapped around her neck and introduced us to her friends. Kevin and his cookies were a big hit. I stayed until Mabel dragged me away at six; I'd promised to go out to dinner with her before her Oriental cooking class. Luckily, Mabel didn't expect me to share her enthusiasm for Oriental cooking any more than she expected me to take up velvet painting.

Sunday hadn't been too productive, but I began in earnest Monday morning with a list of contact people from Alice, whose affiliation with Legal Aid had, as it turned out, proven useful. A week after the murder had been discovered, the cops weren't able to tell me much about the case. Betty Bags had been murdered by a person unknown. She had been killed with her own knife, which she customarily carried in one of her shopping bags. She had taken the bus to Knowlton's Corner in Northside, presumably with the intent to transfer. For some reason, she had instead gone to the Patagonia Arms four blocks away and been murdered. She had entered a locked apartment — the police sergeant managed to sound skeptical even over the phone — and her assailant had locked the door upon leaving. It had taken all my communications skills, honed on more than three decades of experience as a mother, to weasel this much information out of the cop I talked to. I just made it sound like I was sending him to bed without any Jell-O if he didn't tell me the truth.

Nobody knew where Betty's shopping bags were. Nobody knew why her clothes were searched afterward. Nobody knew where the key to the apartment was. Nobody knew why anybody thought she had anything worth stealing. Nobody knew who her next of kin was. Nobody knew why she had ended up on the streets in the first place. Nobody knew her real name. It was depressing as hell.

I started at the Department of Human Services. It was 85 fucking degrees at 9:15, and the receptionist's bleached blonde hair was flapping limply in the breeze from an ancient little fan that sounded like a machine gun on its last round. She told me that Mrs. Murphy, the person Alice had directed me to, was on the phone, and I'd have to wait. I settled into one of those butt-busting hard plastic chairs between a Black woman with three hyperactive kids and a white woman with a squalling baby. A middle-aged Black woman appeared from somewhere behind the receptionist's desk. She was accompanied by a young white couple with an anxious look.

"Now remember," she said briskly. "I need a social security card for each of the children before I can do anything. You get me those social security cards, bring them with you when you come, and then we'll see." She sounded like me telling a young Franny that she'd have to sit on her potty longer if she wanted a Nutty Buddy.

They mumbled their thanks and trudged off. She turned to the receptionist, who handed her a card. "Mr. Metzger?"

An ancient Black gentleman — that's the only word for a guy who would wear a three-piece suit and a hat in 90-degree heat — made his way slowly toward the receptionist's desk.

A muscular middle-aged white man stalked out of the back and nearly knocked him down.

"Fucking forms! Every time I come down here, fucking bitch gives me more fucking forms to fill out! This ain't a welfare office — it's a goddamn holding pen!"

The kids watched him with curiosity. The woman next to me nodded assent.

"It's the truth. You think the gov'mint would want to hep folks out, 'stead of drivin' 'em crazy, treatin' 'em like dirt, and 'vestigatin' 'em as if they was Russian spies."

"The government don't give a rat's ass what happens to us," said the woman with the baby.

"Yeah, but you want to know somethin'?" The other mother lowered her voice conspiratorially. "If it wasn't for us, these women work here at the Welfare, they wouldn't have no job. Be out on the streets, same as us. You think they treat us nicer."

I was becoming interested in the conversation, but I heard my name called. A washed-out woman around my age, with mousy gray hair in a new perm, was looking at me. I stood up, feeling the resentment around me.

"This won't take long," I announced to the group.

As I marched away, I heard the response from my neighbor: "Honey, if you didn't bring your birth certificate, marriage certificate, social security card, tax returns and vaccination papers, it surely won't." Everybody laughed.

"Miss Rosenberg sent you?" She looked at me over her bifocals.

"Yes." I took a deep breath. "I'm investigating the murder of one of the local street people. She went by the name Betty Bags."

"Bags is her name? I don't think I have a client named Mrs. Bags."

This was going to be harder than I thought, though I can't say Alice didn't warn me.

"No, I don't think Bags was her real name. It was just a nickname — because she was a bag lady."

"Well, of course, our clients are all listed by their real names, the names which appear on their social security cards. We can't issue any assistance to anyone under a nickname."

I just remembered a major drawback to my new career choice. I do not suffer fools gladly.

"No, I know that. But I just wondered if anybody here in the office knew her, or worked with her under her real name."

"Well, I wouldn't have any way of knowing that."

"Okay, look, I gather that she wasn't a client of yours, since you don't recognize the name—"

"But I wouldn't have known her by that name."

"Right, but you might have been aware of her nickname. Anyway, you'd know if you had a client named Betty or Elizabeth, assuming that part of her nickname was accurate, who was a very thin, short, elderly woman destitute enough to have been living on the streets."

"Well, of course, if she was actually living on the streets, she couldn't have been a client of ours because she wouldn't have a fixed address. You can't receive public assistance unless you have a fixed address."

I counted to ten.

"Yes, I know you have to have a fixed address to receive welfare, but some people do use an address — a relative's address or a friend's address or even a shelter address — just so they can receive welfare, don't they? They may not actually be living there."

"But they have to be living there. Otherwise it's illegal."

"Right, it's illegal. But people do it, don't they?"

"Some of them may get away with it for a while, but we always catch up with them in the end."

"All right, let's assume that Betty received some kind of public assistance illegally. My goal is to find out whether she did and to talk to the case worker assigned to her."

"Well, it wasn't me."

"I understand. Do you think you could ask around for me, or do I need to make an appointment with every case worker and ask them personally?"

"You know that all of our information is strictly confidential, Mrs.—"

"Caliban."

"—Mrs. Caliban. Even if we have information about Mrs. Bags, we can't release it to a private citizen. We have to protect her privacy."

"But she's dead."

"We still have to protect her privacy." Even she heard how funny this sounded, so she shifted tacks. "If not for her sake, then for the next of kin."

"But nobody knows who the next of kin *is*. That's part of the problem. We're trying to track them down."

"By 'we,' do you mean you and the police?"

"Sort of."

"Well, if the police would make a request through official channels, then perhaps we could do something. Until then, I'm afraid my hands are tied." She flashed me a sour smile.

"Is there a special form they use to make a request like that?" I couldn't help myself.

"Yes, of course. They'll know."

I was still in a snit when I reported in to Kevin. Breakfast for bartenders comes around twelve-thirty, so he was just getting up when I returned from a morning of sleuthing and sweating.

Damn polyester blouse was like a solar panel, and my pantyhose were driving me nuts. I'd bet my last ounce of Chanel No.5 that a man invented pantyhose. I hope he's condemned to wear them in hell; *he'll* see how bloody cool and comfortable they are.

"So you're dining out this evening?"

"Alice thinks that I should go down to the St. Francis Soup Kitchen and talk to Sister Mary Jeanne. If I go at dinner-time, I'll probably get to meet some of Betty's friends.

"Look, I need to work on the key angle. The cops asked you who used to live upstairs, right? That's what I need to know. Also if there was a resident manager, or what."

"I only go back a year and a half."

"So tell me what you know."

"Well, when I moved in, Mrs. Tetley lived upstairs — Annabel. Annabel was in her seventies and had lived in that same apartment for donkey's years, apparently. Then her friend Millie finally talked her into investing in a condo at one of those slick retirement villages, so she packed up her parakeets and departed."

"Which retirement village?"

"Whispering Pines — can you believe it? Just like in Nancy Drew, she told me. Then there was Connie Steinfirst. Connie was a redhead with a figure like Marilyn Monroe in the late fifties. Connie was unlucky in love. Connie was always unlucky in love. She worked downtown in some law office as a secretary and she was always meeting heels, or so she told me. She was on the mend from a broken heart when she moved in, but within a month she had a new friend, the distinguished older type, married. That lasted six months, and when it ended she moved to Los Angeles. She didn't have much hope that her life would change and she would stop attracting louses, but she thought as long as she was going to be miserable, she might as well be miserable in a good climate."

"Do you have her address in case I need it?"

"Yeah, sure. I know she made it to L.A. She sent me a photograph of herself in a hot tub, so it must be true."

"Okay, who's next?"

"Germaine Trudelle. Tall, skinny Black guy who always wore sunglasses. Germaine ran a business out of his home, and his clients trooped up and down the stairs all hours of the day and night. Once when I complained, Germaine offered to cut me in. He figured, me being a bartender and all, I could help him out on distribution. He was that discreet. He stayed four months before he decided to move uptown to a place that would enhance his image. Image was everything to Germaine."

"You got his address?"

"No, but I bet the cops do."

"Okay, who else?"

"That's it. The apartment was vacant after Germaine moved out. By then the Chesters — that was the young couple that lived in your place and managed the building — they were gone, too, and the building was up for sale."

"Were the Chesters here when you came?"

"Yes."

"What were they like? And why did they leave?"

"They were sweet — you know, like straight couples can be. Young love and all that. He worked downtown selling computers and she worked part-time at Burke Marketing. Then they got pregnant and decided to move to the 'burbs and raise a family."

"What's wrong with raising a family in Northside, apart from folks like Germaine? I'm doing it!" I'd had one too many calls from Sharon and Jason since the murder, and I was testy. You'd think I'd moved into the murder capital of the Tri-State.

"Ah, but this is your second time around. You're older and wiser now. Besides, your kids—" Sidney came flying through the air and landed in Kevin's plate. He wrapped his paws around what was left of Kevin's bagel, stood up on his hind legs and batted it as if it were a small furry animal, then took a bite out of its spine. "—Your kids can take care of themselves."

That's my boy. He can beat up any bagel on the goddamn block.

CHAPTER 5

The St. Francis Soup Kitchen was down on West Liberty Street in Over-the-Rhine. You couldn't miss it; it was labeled with a big sign. Looking for nonpaying customers.

The thermometer had dropped to a chilly eighty-three, but I had spent enough time in kitchens in my day not to be fooled by a cold snap. I was wearing a cotton shirtwaist that would have to be ironed sometime this winter or donated to the Freestore. More Donna Reed than Lana Turner. Suitable for interviewing a nun. Sister Mary Jeanne was a short woman who had clearly sampled her wares on a regular basis — the sign of a good chef, in my book. She had a sweet face, flushed from her work. She was in mufti, except for a prominent gold cross around her neck.

I offered to help, so I sliced carrots while she chopped onions. I couldn't tell if she was crying over Betty or the onions, but probably a little of both.

"Really, we're all so very upset about Betty's death. We can't imagine who would have wanted to kill her."

"You don't think she had any enemies?"

"Well, my goodness, *enemies* is such a strong word, isn't it? I don't think I have enemies, but heaven knows I've offended enough people in my day. And Betty was not always as tactful as she might have been. But you see the problem, don't you, Mrs. Caliban? People don't kill you because you've offended them or hurt their feelings. At least, under the circumstances—"

"The circumstances?"

"Well, someone might stab a person in the heat of an argument, don't you see, but in Betty's case — why, she was somewhere she never goes. She was in your apartment. How did she get there?" She paused in her chopping, shifted her knife hand to her hip and looked up at me with wide gray eyes, as if to emphasize her incredulity.

"I mean, it's not as if she argued with someone out here on the sidewalk on West Liberty. It's not as if she had an altercation with someone over something she found in the dumpster on Twelfth Street." She waved the knife, presumably in the direction of a Twelfth Street dumpster. "So she must have had, as you say, an enemy. But who?"

"You don't think she could have owned anything valuable enough to steal? She *was* searched after she was killed, and her shopping bags were stolen."

Sister Mary Jeanne shook her head in wide-eyed disbelief. "She may have had something valuable, or she may not have. Who would know? She was very careful about her things; they all are, and so would you be if everything you had in life was contained in the shopping bags you carried around. Someone would scarcely murder her on the off chance that she had something worth stealing, would they? Unless of course they were crazy, or just downright mean, which amounts to the same thing." She gave the next onion a vicious whack with the knife.

"If we assume that the killer thought she had something he wanted," I said, "something particular, then maybe it was only valuable to him. Suppose she found something — letters or pornographic pictures or something — would she have been capable of blackmail, do you think?"

Sister Mary Jeanne studied her onion.

"Yes, I suppose so. I see what you mean. And I suppose it's possible. You think she arranged to meet somebody to discuss blackmail? And she, or perhaps he (if it was a he), chose Northside rather than Over-the-Rhine to ensure secrecy."

"Something like that. But she had a bus transfer, which means she intended to go somewhere else before heading back downtown. Where do you think she was going?"

"Oh, where she always went on Saturdays, I imagine. To the cemetery."

I got so excited I chopped my fingertip.

"Oh, *sh-oot!*" I said.

* * *

Sister Mary Jeanne guided me to a table where three men were sitting. Let me correct that. One of them, possibly white, was slouched over the table, unconscious, to all appearances. A balding older Black man was sitting. A gray-haired middle-aged Black man was standing. They carried the stamp of poverty on their clothes and their faces, and they smelled about like anybody would have if they had spent twelve hours rummaging through the city's trash in 95-degree heat and then hijacked a whiskey truck on their way to dinner. Or maybe only one of them smelled like the whiskey truck; it was hard to tell.

"Well, Curtis, you're looking chipper, considering the heat." Sister Mary Jeanne addressed the younger Black man. "Someone die and leave you money?"

"Well, I tell you, Sister, this heat be bad for sleepin' but good for business. It ain't nothin' like a good heatwave to make folks spend they money at the canned drink machines. And when it be hot, folks love to drink, and that keep Curtis in the pink. 'Cause every can they throw away be added on to Curtis's pay."

"And if you wise you save that pay, have some left another day," the sitting man joined in. "'Cause winter come, and it be cold, cain't find no tin to turn to gold."

"'Thout no gold, you got no bed, wind up in the streets stone dead."

"And when you dead, here come the Man, and smash you flat like a old tin can."

"They burn you up, you turn to ash, and fall all over the city trash."

"And when you meet the angel Michael, he wearin' a badge say 'We Recycle.'"

The two men ended with a high-five. We applauded. The third man, a grizzled, pale, emaciated individual with grimy black hair, looked up groggily, adjusted his glasses and observed, "You'll be lucky if they don't recycle *you* to one o' them research laboratories at the medical college."

Sister Mary Jeanne broke in to introduce me. The sitting man was named Obie, and the third man was called "Jinks" or "Jinx." I wondered which, but I gave him the benefit of the doubt. She explained that I was looking into Betty's murder and excused herself. Before we got any further, there was an ejaculation from Curtis, who was still standing.

"Lord have mercy, look who's here. It's the honkettes. Whyn't you ladies go find yourself some nice respectable segregated restaurant and leave us poor old darkies in peace?"

A skinny white woman with stringy brown hair and bad teeth slammed her purse down on the table.

"Ain't this one segregated? Shit, I'ma write my congressman."

Trailing behind her were a nervous, frail-looking older woman — by which I mean older even than me — and a tall awkward girl whose eyes looked funny, both of them white. I started trying to remember what I'd learned about drugs. The older woman was toting five shopping bags, which she arranged on either side of her chair.

I was introduced again. The first woman was Trish, the bag lady was Patty, and the space cadet was Zona.

The dinner line opened before our conversation could begin, and by the time they reassembled, we'd been joined by an intense young white man — "call me Steel" — in camouflage and an elderly Black woman named Alma who said very little. When she did speak, she seemed to be addressing Jesus and not us.

"So how come you're interested in Betty?" Steel asked, a touch of something I took for belligerence in his voice.

"She was murdered upstairs from me — in my building."

"So you're scared the killer's gonna come back and get you?"

"Not particularly. But I'm a private investigator, and private investigators don't let innocent people get murdered upstairs." This sounded too Sam Spade, even to me, so I couldn't blame them for staring. Here I was, melting into a cotton shirtwaist that practically screamed "grandma," and I was coming across like a gun thug out of a forties movie. A man's gotta do what a man's gotta do. I put it down to the heat.

"Look," I tried again. "I'm the one that found the body. It really upset me. Plus, it pissed me off."

There was a throaty murmur of assent from Obie, or else a carrot had lodged in his throat.

"It's okay." Curtis waved aside his comrade's suspicions. "We with you. What you want to know? The police already done talked to some of us."

"Shit, the cops don't care shit about us, and you know it," Steel said. "They're too busy bustin' street peddlers and hasslin' hookers to be lookin' for Betty's murderer."

"It's some truf in that." Obie nodded at me. "Cops ax questions, but they don't listen to the answers."

"The cops don't give a shit what happened to Betty." Trish was smoking and eating alternately. "If we's all murdered, they probly give the killer the key to the damn city."

"What do *you* think happened to her?"

Curtis appeared to be the group's spokesperson.

"Tell the truth, we don't know what to think. We figure Betty caught the bus out to Spring Grove that Saturday, like every Saturday. That's where her mama buried — Spring

Grove Cemetery." I nodded. Sister Mary Jeanne had explained this part. "To get there, she have to ride the bus to Knowlton's Corner and transfer. But she didn't do that this time, did she? Instead, she walk a couple blocks to some apartment building, get herself killed. And with her own knife." He shook his head. "No, ma'am, it don't make no kind of sense, noways."

"See, the thing is . . . Betty ain't the kind to get friendly with strangers, see what I mean?" Trish paused to light another cigarette.

"You never know about strangers, and that's a fact." Patty leapt unexpectedly into the breach. "There's so many muggers on the streets these days. And you can't tell by looking at them. They prey on the elderly." Her eyes widened and locked on mine. She knew elderly when she saw it, Sam Spade repartee or no.

"That's what Betty thought, anyway. She was suspicious of everybody." Trish studied the end of her cigarette.

Jinks, who was snoring into his soup, opened one eye and said, "A body can't be too suspicious."

"So, anyway, why would Betty walk away from Knowlton's Corner unless she was lured away? And who'd be able to convince her to go with him? It don't make sense."

"Maybe she was kidnapped by aliens." This was Zona's first contribution.

"Yeah, and maybe I'm Roy Rogers," Obie said.

"Well, I read in this paper at Kroger's where this couple from Gary, Indiana, was kidnapped by aliens, and—"

"Zona, honey, get a grip," Trish said. "If it was aliens, they wouldn't have to kill her with her own knife. They got ray guns and lasers and shit."

"Did you all know about the knife?"

"Half of Cincinnati knew about the knife. She thought anybody was gettin' too close to her, or lookin' too hard at her bags, or infringin' on her territory, why, she got hysterical. I ain't never seen her pull that knife on nobody, but she be threatenin' 'em with it at the top of her lungs."

"Sure, she was all the time creatin' a disturbance. Cops got used to it. 'I got a knife!' she say. 'They try to steal anything from me and I'll use it, too!' Cops say, 'Sure, sure, Betty. We know you will. But you keep it put away for now so nobody gets hurt.'"

"It was a combat knife, like the ones we used in 'Nam," Steel offered. "She got it at an army surplus store."

"What did you mean, Curtis, when you said somebody might be infringing on Betty's territory? Do you mean her collecting territory?"

"That's right. Some folks get to workin' a street or a neighborhood so long, they come to see it as they territory. They figure they get the first pick — like on trash day, and all. Some folks get mighty provoked if they think somebody else is movin' in. Betty was like that."

"What would her territory have been?"

"Oh, say, Findlay Market south 'bout ten blocks, east, maybe three blocks. Right in there. Course, Findlay is fair game for everybody, 'cause the pickin's is good on market days. Like Globe Furniture, right there on the corner. The furniture boxes come in real handy in the wintertime."

"I *still* say it was Edgar-goddamn-Kirkendahl and his hired thugs that got her." Steel pounded the table for emphasis.

"Aw, man, what you want to go confuse the issue for? What they want with Betty? Just 'cause she a member of Street People United don't make her worth killin'."

"Yeah, if they was going after SPU, they'da killed McGann, not Betty."

"What's Street People United?" I asked, my ears pricking.

"It's a organization we all belong to."

"Not me." Jinks didn't even open his eyes.

"'Scuse me, a organization that everybody but Jinks belong to. Run by a white dude name of Bill McGann. He want to get us organized so we can get us some more shelters and services."

"Did he have anything to do with the sit-in in that vacant building on 14th Street not too long ago?"

"That's right! We were there!" Obie said excitedly.

"Those motherfucking capitalist pigs own real estate all over downtown, half of it sitting empty," Steel spat. "But they wouldn't want to provide shelter for street people, oh, no. It might ruin their goddamn property value."

"And Betty was a member? Did she attend the sit-in?"

"Yeah, she was there. Bill like her, too. He say it good for the cause to have a old woman gettin' dragged out of a building on the six o'clock news. Trouble was she was always so moufy. Kinda spoilt the effect to have her cussin' the police at the top of her lungs. Couldn't use no sound at all on that tape."

I liked Betty better all the time. My kind of woman. But what did I know about her?

"Anybody know anything about Betty's background? Where she came from? Whether she had any relatives? Anything like that?"

"She never mentioned no relatives," Trish said. "If she had family, she never seen 'em. I ain't never heard nothin' about her background. Not really."

"'You shoulda seen me when I was young, dearie,'" Zona said in an eerie, languid voice that was a real conversation stopper. "'I had the prettiest skin and the prettiest eyes you ever saw. I wore diamonds and pearls, and danced the Charleston all night long. I coulda had my pick of dozens of men, dozens of 'em. They fought to drink champagne outta my shoe.' *That's* what she said to me once."

"*A-men*," said Alma.

"Well," Trish said hesitantly, "sometimes when she'd been drinking, she talked like that, but we didn't believe half of it, you know. Even if it was true, look where she ended up."

"She been around long as I been around," said Obie, "which mean she been around longer than me."

"She used to collect welfare, up until about a month ago. Some motherfuckin' narc tipped 'em off she was collecting at a house over on Lincoln Avenue, and she didn't really have no goddamned fixed address. Dude on Lincoln Avenue's a minister, belongs to SPD, he was helping her out. And the bastard she blamed was Edgar-goddamn-Kirkendahl."

"Do you know how she happened to end up on the streets?"

"No. But if you ax me, she been in the hospital some times. You know, up to Hotel Ohio. She talk like she have."

"That's right," said Steel, who looked like the voice of authority on this matter. "We talked once about the drugs they give you."

"But she hasn't been in since you've known her," I said to Obie. "I mean, she hasn't disappeared from the streets for a while." He shook his head.

"Well, I feel like I'm gathering lots of information about her, but I still don't have much of a sense of what she was like as a person."

"She wasn't easy to get along with, but neither are we." Curtis was answering. "She could be suspicious, mean, spiteful, but then again she could be generous, help somebody along. She was smart — you could see that. She was mad all the time, at somebody or somethin' made her life turn out the way it did. We know all about that. What difference it make what she was like? She was a person, now she dead. Ain't nobody got the right to do that to her."

I thought about something Sister Mary Jeanne had said.

"You know," she'd said, "I think you're just the right person to solve Betty's murder. Lots of people, police and press included, think, 'Why fuss over one old lady's death?' She was eighty-something anyway, and we've all got to go sometime. She'd been on the street for years. It's a miracle she survived as long as she did. But you and I see things differently. It wasn't Betty's time. Somebody took away from her whatever time she had left. That's a terrible crime."

Trish was talking again.

"You best go see Lucille. Lucille knows more about her than anybody."

"Lucille?"

"Shit, ain't we mentioned Lucille? Lucille was Betty's best friend. She must be devastated now. Hey, Alma!" Alma looked startled and turned her head. "You seen Lucille lately?"

"Lucille? Lucille Shelton? Ain't seen her. Ain't seen her nor that skinny little white woman she run with." She looked down at her soup. "'Let me die the death of the righteous, and let my last end be like hers!'"

Well, this made me feel pretty creepy, I can tell you, but Trish just said "Amen" and kept right on talking to me. "Lucille Shelton is her name. Black lady Betty's age."

"How would I find her?"

"We ain't seen her around lately, so I 'magine she's visitin' to her cousin's. But I don't know where her cousin live at. Up on the hill past Liberty, I believe."

Jinks had opened his eyes, both of them. He was staring at me.

"Where's Lucille disappeared to?" he said. "Why don't you investigate that?"

CHAPTER 6

Well, shit, I felt like I'd been asked to feed the neighbors' cat while they were away, and I'd gone to the door and called "kitty" and every damn cat in the neighborhood came running. How was I going to know which one to feed? I'd have to feed them all, just to make sure the right one got her dinner.

So I'd gone looking for a little information to help solve the bag lady murder. And I'd figured information would be hard to come by. Now I had clues of all kinds, crowding up against me, butting their heads against my ankles. How did I know which one was a real clue?

First, there was the key business. A skilled person could have opened the locked apartment door without a key; my research had progressed that far, at least. But how many burglars locked the door behind them as they left?

Besides, I couldn't imagine Betty being lured to some strange apartment and then standing around whistling Dixie while the lurer worked on the lock. Of course, he didn't have to worry about her standing around afterward, but still. And who the hell was he, anyway? He couldn't have been just some guy in a lab coat who stepped up to her with a clipboard and asked if she'd participate in a consumer survey. She would have sliced and diced his survey into confetti.

So either he looked like some kind of authority figure — say, a cop — or he was somebody she knew. And I didn't really trust the authority figure line, because I didn't think she would. I already felt that Betty would have fought to the death to defend her bags, even from a cop. But who did she know? The guys at the soup kitchen? Jinks? This McGann guy, the organizer? Did he kill her because she wouldn't take out a sustaining membership in SPU? Or the real estate mogul — what was his name? Kirkendahl? Did he bump her off welfare? Did she plot revenge against him because she thought he had, and did it go wrong somehow? I wrote myself a little note to check and see if he had ever owned the ol' Catatonia Arms.

Probably, this Street People United business was just the infamous red herring — or maybe I should say the Cheshire cat, just to keep my metaphors consistent. I remembered something about them. They had occupied a vacant building in one demonstration, demanding that the owner open it up to house the homeless. And I'd gotten a shiver down my spine when Curtis said what he'd said about the six o'clock news. Because I realized that I'd *seen* Betty Bags when she was alive. She was being dragged off by two blue boys, her bags bumping along the ground, her mouth working like an auctioneer's. And she was *pissed*. No, I couldn't see her trailing along behind a cop to discuss anything with him: "Why, certainly, officer. I'd be happy to give you a few minutes of my time."

On the other hand, what if the murderer was a woman? Probably I should find out more about the medical evidence, since in the novels they were always talking about the strength behind the thrust and shit like that. Murder by women, after all, had been known to happen: look at Lizzie Borden. Jean Harris didn't count, in my book. I considered that justifiable homicide, and if you've ever been on the Scarsdale diet, you know what I mean. Anybody who says she never contemplated the pleasure of blasting that self-righteous bastard to kingdom come is leaving the cream out of her Oreos.

It's always hard to imagine a woman killing another woman in cold blood, though. Did I think Trish could do it? Patty? Zona was living on another planet, so I left her out of my deliberations. This crime was carefully planned. I was willing to nominate the ice lady from the Welfare Office, but I didn't think she'd know how to get her period without a requisition form, much less freelance as a murderer.

That brought me to Lucille Shelton, Betty's best friend. How come nobody had seen her around lately? Was she visiting her cousin, or was she on the lam? Could I think of a reason why a woman might skewer her best friend? Well, I could think of a few, but they didn't seem applicable. Sexual jealousy? Sartorial jealousy? See what I mean?

In fact, motive seemed to be the one cat that hadn't shown its whiskers yet. Was Betty toting around the Hope diamonds in the bottom of her bag, tangled up in the loose shoestrings? Or was she carrying the clandestine correspondence of the city's respected officials or beloved sports figures? Was she dealing coke like a migratory medicine man? Was she the last of the long-lost heirs to an obscure fortune to be standing between her murderer and multi-millionairedom? Was she herself an eccentric multimillionaire who preferred the freedom of open spaces to life in the family mansion in Hyde Park?

And while we're on the subject of mansions, how had the murder been planned? When, exactly, did it take place? The bus transfer was stamped 1:40 p.m., but could we then assume that Betty walked right to the apartment and was killed? Maybe she had stopped to shop at the army surplus store. The transfer seemed to suggest that she had been killed *after* 1:40, but it may have been a clever plant by somebody who had an alibi then. I'd read too many mysteries in my day to fall for the old ticket-proves-time-of-death routine.

Kevin and I both get up late on Saturdays, and anybody could figure that out, though it gave me the creeps to admit it. Kevin swears that if he'd been home when the murder was committed, he would have heard something, but I don't know. That goddamn air conditioner purrs like the Incredible Shrinking Man's cat. And I don't think *I* would have heard anything over my own snores. Later on, Kevin had gone out to play tennis, like he does every other Saturday, and I went to the grocery store, like I do every Saturday. If the murder was committed then — and I confess I lean toward the reassuring possibility that I wasn't around when it happened — somebody either counted on our going out or got lucky. In general, I thought of the murderer as a lucky guy. But I didn't think he was *that* lucky.

Things looked better after my second gin and tonic. Nothing had changed but my perspective — which was, admittedly, getting blurred around the edges. I had a lot of cats to feed, but before I wasted too much more time, I thought I needed to try the obvious. *Had* anybody spotted Betty walking with her murderer that morning? What I needed was a snap of Betty, and I doubted it was going to be easy to come by. She wasn't the photogenic type.

I called Alice Rosenberg upstairs. By now I was reclining in the bathtub, bubble bath up to my earlobes, G&T number three on the edge of the tub, the telephone cord stretched taut from the next room like a clothesline for pixies. This sleuthing shit really takes a lot out of you.

Alice said the cops would at least have a photograph of the corpse. I asked whether she had any pull with the police that she would like to exercise in a worthy cause. She said she worked for Legal Aid, and the police hated her guts. Actually, she put it more politely than that, but that's what she meant. She said I should call Marge Kleindienst at the Freestore.

I rang Marge's number. I was playing with the tap with my big toe, making like I was a tap dancer, wondering if it was really possible to get your toe stuck in the faucet the way Laura Petry did on the "Dick Van Dyke Show." Marge answered, a cheery voice, eager to be helpful — the kind of person who should have been working at the Welfare Office. She had a connection, all right, and she'd see what she could do for me. She couldn't add much to what I'd already learned about Betty, but she did know Lucille and thought she might have an address for Lucille's family. She'd call me the next afternoon.

I hung up, dripping all over the phone and the floor, and reached for the Orania Papazoglou mystery I was reading. I sank back down in the water with a sigh of contentment. Sophie, the gray tiger, was sitting on the edge of the tub like a statue.

"Another day, another dollar," I told her.

* * *

The next morning I was working on my yoga when the doorbell rang. It was a plainclothes cop named Eddie Landau. He'd gone to high school with Marge's sister. Eddie brought me two photographs in a plain brown envelope. Who says there's never a cop around when you need one?

"If anybody asks where you got 'em, just say a reporter gave 'em to you."

Apparently, Betty had been booked for vagrancy or D&D at some point, so the first was a set of black-and-white mug shots. The way she looked at the camera, you would've thought the lens would shatter. It was more than a little weird to look her in the eye for the first time. It made me feel like she was pissed at me for not catching her murderer.

The other was, as Marge had predicted, a headshot of Betty, dead. This one was color, but she had her eyes closed. The headshot info said her eyes were brown, but the first pictures made them look black. All in all, I hoped that somewhere, somehow, a more sympathetic, more flattering picture of Betty existed. She did not look like a happy woman.

"Marge said to give you any help you needed on accounta this old — uh, this lady — was a pal of hers."

"Do they have a real identification on her yet?" I'd noticed that the photos said "Betty Bags."

"Nah, they'll probably never find out who she was, really. These bag ladies — unless they got some family they still keep in touch with — they've mostly lost their past along the way, you know? I mean, they ain't gonna show up in the FBI fingerprint files for carrying stolen garbage across state lines."

"I'm also interested in a friend of hers — Lucille Shelton. She hasn't been seen on the streets since Betty was killed, and she *did* have family in town. Do you think you could check and see if the family has filed a Missing Persons on her?"

He nodded and laboriously wrote her name in pencil on a small notepad.

He had his hand on the door when I thought of something else.

"Have you heard of a group called Street People United?"

"Sure, I heard of 'em. Hell, we busted some of 'em a month ago."

"How are they perceived in the police department?"

"Well, let me put it this way. They're a pain in the ass, but next to Right to Life, they're a minor-league pain in the ass, know what I mean? Lotta guys on the force sympathize with 'em. Hell, there's plenty of vacant buildings around. Seems kinda dumb to lock people up in jail if all's they need's a place to sleep."

"What about Bill McGann?"

"Aw, Bill's okay. He's a hothead, but like I say, a lotta guys think he's on the right track."

"And Edgar Kirkendahl? What do they think of him?"

"Well, I ask you, how many guys on the force you think own a couple million dollars' wortha downtown real estate? Our job's to protect property, but there's property — and there's property. Kirkendahl runs around acting like he owns the goddamn city. Thinks District One is his own private security force. Rubs people the wrong way. If it was up to us, shit, we'd let people sleep in his empty buildings. Let me put it this way: nobody ever asked him to play Santa Claus at the orphans' Christmas party."

So I bumped Edgar-goddamn-Kirkendahl to the top of my list of murder suspects.

I put on shorts of a respectable length and a plaid cotton shirt, and my Adidas. It doesn't do to intimidate folks in

Northside. I strolled down to Hamilton Avenue and started at Knowlton's Corner, the side of the street where Betty's bus had stopped. I struck out at the printer's on the corner — they're closed Saturdays anyway — and at the Food Co-op next door. You'd think all those organically grown veggies would sharpen their eyesight and their memory, but it doesn't. No luck either at La Pooch Designer T-shirts or the beauty shop. Len's Lounge brought me my first piece of luck.

You wouldn't think there'd be so many people drinking in semi-darkness in the late morning on a weekday in the summer. You don't know Northside. Ten people, mostly older men, crowded around to study Betty's pictures. She looked sorta like somebody's second cousin. She had a nose like the sportscaster on Channel 12, a chin like the bartender's niece. But no, nobody had seen Betty herself.

"You ask Leon Jakes?"

"Who's Leon?"

"Shit, you don't know who Leon is? How long you say you lived in Northside?"

The room exploded, everyone talking at once.

"Once, I remember Leon went to the store for his mother and came home with . . ." "I recollect the time Leon . . ." "And so I asked Leon, I said . . ." "And Leon looked at his brother, and he said, 'I may be retarded, but I ain't stupid!'"

Leon, it seemed, was a Northside character, a mentally handicapped kid who earned a living doing odd jobs for businesses up and down Hamilton Avenue. Whatever his limitations, he had clearly carved out a niche for himself. Folks laughed a lot and shook their heads when they told Leon stories, but beneath the laughter was respect. Leon was Somebody.

"Whyn't you go across the street to Ed's and see if he's working there today? He'll be around somewhere, and if anybody spotted your bag lady, it would be Leon."

I found Leon washing dishes at Ed's. Tall, skinny Black kid with a physique that looked a lot like Abraham Lincoln's. Big hands. Sleepy black eyes with long lashes. He was wearing jeans and a T-shirt. The T-shirt looked like a La Pooch second: it said "Ralph's Readi-Bowlf."

I explained to him that I was trying to find someone who had seen a certain woman get off the bus at Knowlton's Corner two Saturdays ago. I thought perhaps she had met someone and walked up Knowlton with him or her.

Leon studied the mug shots blankly. Then I showed him the other photo.

"What wrong with her?" He pointed. He might be mentally handicapped but he knew a corpse when he saw one.

"She's dead. I think the person she was walking with might have killed her."

He nodded. "Yes, ma'am, I s-seen her."

"You did? When?"

He looked at me like he thought I was a little slow. "When you say."

My heart began to do the Bristol stomp against my ribcage. "Saturday before last?"

He nodded. "Uh-huh."

"Tell me where you were and what you saw."

"I were at C-Cecil's—"

"The locksmith?"

"Uh-huh, Saturdays, I work for Mr. Cecil. I were sweeping the s-sidewalk, when the bus come by."

"And this woman got off."

"Don't know. I only seen the b-bus."

Leon was going to make a star witness. Since the bus had been coming toward him, of course he wouldn't have seen who got off; the bus would have obscured his vision.

"What time was this?"

"Maybe, 'b-bout two o'clock."

Right on the money. "Okay, so what happened next?"

"It was a lady — *this* lady — come across the street with a man."

"Was she carrying anything?" Cagey, Cat, very cagey. Leading the witness.

"S-seem like she have a whole mess of bags, like shoppin' bags."

"And did you see the man she was with?"

"Uh-huh."

"What did he look like?"

"He have on a Reds cap, like the one my b-brother Junior give me for my b-birthday, and sunglasses."

My spirits sank. "What else?"

"Jeans, and a Reds T-shirt, and gym shoes."

A devilishly clever disguise. It wouldn't work in Cleveland, maybe, or Pittsburgh, but in Cincinnati nobody would look twice at an average Joe in a Reds T-shirt and cap.

"So I guess you wouldn't recognize him if you saw him again?"

"Yes, ma'am, I would." My heart took a breather.

"You *would*?"

"Yes, ma'am."

"But he had on sunglasses."

"Yes, ma'am, but they fell off when the l-lady hit him."

"She *hit* him?" I'd like to think of Betty going down swinging.

"Yes, ma'am, as they come up on the c-curb, he reach out like he goin' to take her arm, and she p-punch him in the stomach."

Betty didn't want anybody to get that close, and she wasn't accustomed to gentlemanly gestures. So when the bastard made one, she slugged him. Better and better.

"So what did he look like?"

This question stumped my exemplary witness.

"Well, was he tall, short, or average? Fat or thin? Black, white, or otherwise? Did he have a big nose? A long nose? Thin lips? Any scars?"

"He w-wasn't that tall. Shorter than me, little bit." Since Leon was pushing six feet, I recognized that we were going to have a problem with his points of reference. "He was a white man."

Silence.

"What color were his eyes?" Not much point in asking about hair if he was wearing a cap.

Silence. Leon's face screwed up in concentration. "If I seed him again, I would know."

This seemed to be a position statement, and I suspected that I would get no further probing for details. I didn't doubt Leon's powers of perception, but his verbal skills left something to be desired. Still, I had a real, bona fide witness. Now I was looking for a man in a Cincinnati Reds cap. If he wasn't the murderer, he knew more about what had happened that Saturday than I did.

I gave Leon a ten-dollar bill.

"I don't think M-Mama would want me to take no money."

"Trust me, Leon, it's okay. We detectives always pay our informants. Union policy."

"B-but I don't belong to no union."

Smarts are relative. You had to get up early in the morning to fool Leon Jakes. I was counting on it.

* * *

"So, you going to tell the cops about Leon?"

Kevin and I were up in Number 4 doing what we do best: drinking beer and watching someone else work. Melanie and Alice had become Mel and Al — the boys, in Kevin's parlance. They didn't seem to object. They liked Kevin. The normally reticent Mel had told me calmly, "If I thought he was trying to insult us, I'd break his neck."

Mel was building a bookshelf. Alice was handing her the nails. Kevin and I were giving her support. I'd learned about the importance of support when Franny had been a counseling major at Wisconsin.

I took a slug of beer and shook my head.

"Let them find their own damn witnesses. Besides, they'd just take him downtown to look through their scrapbooks. I think he could study mug shots till the cows come home, and he wouldn't find the murderer. Unless, of course, this was a drug-related crime."

"At least you have a better picture of your suspect, Mrs. C. I mean, it has to be someone Betty would be willing to go with — someone who could divert her from continuing on to the cemetery. But it wasn't someone she especially trusted or liked, or she wouldn't have taken a swing at him.

"How long are bus transfers good for?" Kevin asked. "An hour, isn't that right, Mel?"

Melanie, her teeth studded with nails, nodded.

"So she could have planned to meet this guy, but she obviously didn't expect the meeting to last very long."

"Or the bus transfer could be the infamous red herring."

"You mean, like resetting the clock and then breaking it? Something to mislead us about the time of death? But it would be hard to fake, wouldn't it? Wouldn't he have had to get the transfer himself at the time stamped on it?"

"I don't know." I sighed. "I suppose I could ask Eager Eddie if the cops compared the stamp to a real one. But I don't suppose a stamp like that would be impossible to fake, if you put your mind to it. And if this guy really needed an alibi, he might have gone to some trouble."

"Yeah, but what I don't get is this," Al said. "Did he intend to kill her or didn't he? He killed her with her own knife, which doesn't indicate that he planned it very well."

"But maybe he planned to strangle her, until she pulled the knife on him," Kevin speculated. "Or maybe he had a gun, and then realized that the knife would provide less evidence. Or maybe he had a gun and planned all along to make her hand over the knife, so he could use it."

"Anyway, all of what we've said so far assumes that the man Leon saw was the murderer, and while I admit that it seems pretty likely, you know that in mystery novels that person always turns out to be perfectly innocent," I warned them.

"In mystery novels," said Mel, "the author does that to complicate the plot. We're dealing with a murderer, not an author."

CHAPTER 7

Marge called that evening with an address for Lucille Shelton's cousin, Sophronia Hewlett. She apologized for not having called earlier; she had had a hectic day. She couldn't give me a phone number for Sophronia and doubted that the Hewletts had a phone anyway. She hoped Eddie had been helpful and encouraged me to take advantage of his agreement to cooperate.

To tell the truth, I didn't feel much like going out again that night, but a detective's lot is not always an easy one, as I was beginning to find out. The thermometer had plummeted to 78, so I put on my jeans and sneaks and set out again for Over-the-Rhine. If Sophronia worked regular daytime hours, I needed to catch her at home tonight.

The address proved to be a dilapidated tenement on Sycamore, across Liberty and up the hill. The smell of hot grease and onions was in the air, and I got some funny looks from the folks sitting out on the front steps, though they all returned my greeting. I rang the bell marked "Hewlett" several times. Given the general condition of the building, I didn't have a hell of a lot of confidence that the button was connected to anything.

"Who you lookin' for, miss?" said a woman from the top step.

"I'm looking for Sophronia Hewlett. Do you know if she's home?"

The step sitters consulted each other and decided that they didn't know whether she was home or not. Had I rung the bell?

"Does the bell work?"

"Well, now, sometimes it do, and then again, sometimes it don't," a short man said with a smile. "Peewee, whyn't you run upstairs for the lady and see if Sophronia home?"

A kid about eight years old got up and disappeared up the stairs.

"Actually, the person I'm looking for is Lucille Shelton. Do any of you know her?"

"Oh, sure, we all know Miss Lucille. What you want with her?"

I really had their attention now. I could tell that I wouldn't get any more information until I clarified my status. If I came to announce that Lucille had won the lottery, that was one thing, but if I came to collect a bill or check her residency status, they wouldn't give me the time of day.

"A friend of hers was murdered about two weeks ago. Maybe you heard about it? Her friend goes by the name Betty Bags. I'm investigating the murder, and I wanted to talk to Lucille to see if she had any ideas about it."

I tried to cast my mission in as positive a light as I could, but I could see they were torn. Murder meant cops and courts, and they weren't sure that Miss Lucille wanted anything to do with either. On the other hand, if the victim was a friend, maybe Miss Lucille would want to be involved. And I sure didn't look like a cop. They asked, just to make sure.

"You a cop?"

"No, I'm a private investigator. Betty was murdered in my building, and I'd like to find the bastard that did it."

This statement elicited some satisfied murmurs. The boy returned and announced that nobody was home upstairs.

"Seem like I seen Miss Lucille three, maybe four days ago."

"That's right. She was staying with Sophronia. I seen her, too, when I went up to borry some sugar. I thought then she didn't look so good. I say, 'Miss Lucille, how you been keepin'?' She say, 'Not so good,' and it was Sophronia told me about her friend being killed. I felt real bad for her, 'cause Betty come by here sometimes, and I talked to her once or twice."

"That's right, miss. We all knew Betty, just to pass the time of day. We seen her with Miss Lucille. Them two was real close."

"Has anybody seen Miss Lucille since yesterday?" Nobody had.

"Well, I guess I'll have to come back. Can I leave a name and phone number with somebody to give to Lucille if you see her?"

They told me that Sophronia worked during the day at a laundry downtown and took my number.

I was feeling frustrated. Hell, I had never been a patient woman — a major character flaw in an aspiring detective. But I worried about Lucille Shelton. I didn't like it that nobody had seen her lately. I didn't like it at all.

* * *

The following afternoon, Eager Eddie called to tell me that Lucille Shelton's body had been found in a dumpster in an alley off Main Street. She'd been stripped to her underwear and strangled, though Eddie couldn't tell me whether she'd been stripped before or after death, but her clothes had been found in the dumpster as well. Her shopping bags had not been found; I asked.

"To tell you the truth, we still wouldn't know who she was if you hadn't asked me to check Missing Persons for her. She looked like she'd been on the streets — the coroner can tell that kind of thing, y'know. But she coulda been anybody. I looked at the name you gave me, and we tracked down her cousin, and the cousin identified the body and clothes. Anyway, I'm supposed to tell you that Sergeant Fricke is very eager to talk to you."

"Likewise, I'm sure. He there now?"

He was, so I hopped in the beige bomber and headed down to the Investigations Bureau. If you've never been inside a police station, you aren't missing much, take it from me. It must have been the last place in the city where the nonsmoking area was smaller than the smoking area. Come to think of it, I never did see a nonsmoking area.

I was ushered into Fricke's office and sat down in an ancient wooden swivel-type desk chair that creaked when I breathed. It was also a real bum-breaker, but I was determined to tough it out. I didn't want anybody thinking the old lady couldn't take it. Across from me, Sergeant Fricke in shirtsleeves was leaning on the edge of his desk, just like in the movies. He was chewing gum, which didn't make him look any brighter. Eddie was sitting on my right, taking notes. From what I'd seen of his note-taking skills, I figured we were in for a long session.

"Officer Landau tells me you were asking about Lucille Shelton. Thought she might turn up missing. Why were you looking for her?"

I bit back my sarcasm. "She was Betty Bags's best friend. I wanted to ask her about Betty's murder."

He chewed in silence and studied me.

"Okay, leave us ignore for the moment the obvious fact that the Bags murder is police business. Why did you think that Lucille Shelton knew something about it?"

"I didn't know whether she did or not. Just seemed like a good idea when somebody gets murdered to go ask their best friend if they know who did it." I planned to stop here, but my tongue kept moving. "Did you talk to Lucille?"

"So you didn't have no special reason to think Lucille had information about the murder?" He sounded a shade more surly, so I took that to be a no.

"Not at first, but I thought it was suspicious that Lucille had dropped out of sight. Didn't you?"

"You got any other suspicions you want to tell us about before we find another stiff in a dumpster?"

"That was no stiff, that was Miss — or Mrs. — Lucille Shelton," I said icily.

I leaned over and looked him in the eye, the way I looked at my kids when they tracked mud on my clean floor with their brand-new sneakers. "I don't give a shit how many dead bodies you handle in the course of a week. You will call *that* one by her real name, and show her some respect, or I'll ask Howard Ain to investigate why the police department doesn't lift a finger to solve murders when the victims are street people."

Howard Ain was the Channel 12 "troubleshooter." He went around sticking his camera in people's faces and asking them embarrassing questions and generally making himself obnoxious. The threat to sic Howard on Sergeant Fricke was the inspiration of a moment, but it wasn't a bad idea.

Sergeant Fricke turned the color of ripe watermelon. "Who said we hadn't lifted a finger?"

"You got an autopsy report on Betty Bags?"

"Not yet. Not like we need to know the cause of death."

"This is *murder*, for chrissakes!" I threw up my hands in exasperation, and he flinched. I gave myself five points for intimidating a police officer. "Don't you normally expedite an autopsy in a murder case? Do you know for sure whether or not she was drugged before she was stabbed? Did the coroner tell you how strong somebody would have to be to inflict the kind of stab wound she received? Whether it was likely to have been inflicted by a left-handed or right-handed person? How tall? Do you know whether she had a fatal condition that might inspire somebody to eighty-six her before she could change her will?" I didn't even know if Betty had a will, much less anything to leave anybody, but I was on a roll. I figured he had an autopsy report buried somewhere on his desk and hadn't bothered to read it yet.

"Look, Mrs. Caliban, I know all this is pretty new to you and I think it's great you want to start a new career at your age—" He'd switched to patronizing me, the bastard, and he'd just pushed the wrong button.

"What does my goddamn age have to do with your fucking incompetence in conducting a murder investigation? You think because Betty was a bag lady with no identifiable family that nobody gives a shit who killed her and why, so you don't have to? And maybe, just maybe, you think because Betty was an old lady and would've died soon anyway, it doesn't matter. I know you guys got your hands full, sitting on your asses at White Castle and Daily Donuts, waiting for the pushers to show up, ticketing jaywalkers down by the university, policing rock concerts. But *this* old lady is here to tell you that if you think you can get by with ignoring Betty Bags, and now Lucille Shelton, because nobody cares about them, you are wrong. And if you don't have a fucking autopsy report on Lucille Shelton by tomorrow night, you better be ready to defend your badge."

He glared at me, but he'd probably been trained not to slug old ladies. His jaw froze. He cocked his head at the door.

"Beat it."

Effective, but not very original, I thought. I gave him a long look and beat it.

* * *

Two hours later, Eddie Landau called. I was drinking a beer and watching a rerun of a rerun of a show that had originally aired in 1967. I love summer television.

"Man, was he stewed!"

"Are you speaking of my nemesis, Sergeant Fricke, by any chance?"

"Nemesis" was a tricky word to produce after two beers and a long, hard day, but I thought it turned out okay. Even the jaw muscles slow down when you get older.

"I guess I should warn you he said you'd get your P.I. license over his dead body."

"Fine by me, but probably too much to hope for. The question is, did he *do* anything?"

"Yeah, that's what I called to tell you. He's put a rush on the Shelton autopsy, 'in case the old bitch makes good on her threat to call in that asshole Ain,' he said. Report should be in tomorrow."

"Did he find one on Betty?"

"Yeah, but it don't say much. Died of stab wounds administered by a person taller than she was, which covers most of the people of Cincinnati. The perp used her own knife."

"Well, I hope to God you guys searched the dumpster at least."

"Sure, we searched it. Didn't find nothing, though. No shopping bags, no crack, nothing except her clothes. And nothing of Betty's, as far as we could tell, in case you was going to ask."

"I was. Did the coroner or whoever signed the death certificate think she'd been killed right there?"

"He says no."

"Were you there when Fricke talked to the cousin, Sophronia Hewlett?"

"Yep, but she couldn't tell us much. Said Shelton had come to stay with her about two weeks ago, seemed upset about her friend's death."

"'Upset'? Was that all?"

"That's what she thought. Figured Shelton was afraid there was some pervert running around killing old women. Seemed a sensible enough fear for her to have, so Hewlett didn't think much of it. Said she could stay with her as long as she wanted. But here's the funny thing: Hewlett said Shelton didn't go out much at all after she came to stay. Says she stayed holed up in the house."

"So she was afraid of something — or somebody."

"Looks that way."

"Did Lucille ever discuss Betty's death at any length?"

"Hewlett says no. Says people offered their condolences, and she said she just wanted to remember the good times."

This caught me unprepared. I realized I'd gotten in the habit of assuming that street people didn't have "good times," or at least not the kind they think back on sentimentally. There was something else too, though, like a cat taking a swipe at the coattails of my brain and snagging its claws.

"How long had they known each other, Betty and Lucille?"

"Hewlett doesn't know exactly, but she knows it was a long time."

"What kind of a long time? You mean like, ever since Betty went on the streets?"

"No, longer than that, apparently. But Hewlett couldn't seem to explain how or when Lucille ended up on the streets, or where she'd met Betty originally."

No, I hadn't expected that. Not that Black and white women of my generation or older couldn't have been friends, but Cincinnati didn't exactly throw them together.

How had they met if they hadn't met on the streets? Church Women United? The PTA? No, that wouldn't work. Schools weren't really integrated in those days, not really. The YWCA?

"Did Lucille have family — besides Sophronia, I mean?"

"Nah, no kids, Hewlett says. Parents died years ago."

"Yeah? How old was Lucille?"

"Her cousin says early eighties, she's not exactly sure. Look, before you ask me any more questions, why don't you just talk to Hewlett? I think she wants to talk to you."

He was right. Five minutes after he hung up, Sophronia Hewlett called. So once again, I kissed the kitties good-bye (those that were around to be kissed) and headed for Over-the-Rhine. I was wearing this short little bike skirt and a pair of high-heeled sandals. I looked like Betty Grable dressed for dance practice, give or take forty years.

Sophronia Hewlett was paper thin and obsidian black, with the bones of a model and a permanent worry crease across her forehead. She was dressed in a yellow cotton shirtwaist. I was ready to swear that her figure had never seen maternity, but she claimed three of the five junior whirlwinds circulating through the small apartment as hers and told me that the baby was asleep.

"You were awfully generous to share your small apartment with your cousin. Did she stay with you often?"

"Not too often. She could see it was hard, with the kids and just the two rooms. You got kids?"

"Yeah, but they're all grown up."

"Well, you know how it is. I didn't like to think of Cousin Lucille out on the streets, and I swear I'd starve before I'd let one of my family go hungry. But she always said, 'Honey, don't you worry none about me. The Lord will look after me.'" She stopped to sniffle and steady her voice. "I guess the Lord had something else in store for her. But, anyway, she bought food stamps from a lady she knew, and she had a little money from Cousin James — that's her husband — from his life insurance. She always said she could get a place if she wanted, but she was used to her life the way it was. Well, I don't know if she could've gotten a place or not, but that's what she said."

"How long had she known Betty?"

"You know, I can't tell you that. I didn't really know Lucille growing up — not till I moved here. But they went way back, though, those two. Both from Cincinnati, so maybe they knew each other growing up somehow. They were two peas in a pod, like my grandmother would say. Not so much in temperament — Lucille was quiet, and Betty was kindly boisterous. But they understood each other, those two. They didn't talk much about the past, or at least, not in my hearing. Sometimes I think they shared lots of secrets, and they were both real private ladies."

"Do you know Betty's last name?"

She shook her head. "The police asked me that, too. Now isn't that a terrible thing? I saw her lots of times, knew she was Cousin Lucille's best friend, and still I can't say what her name was. Maybe I heard it sometime, I don't know. I've been racking my brain to remember."

"Maybe it will come to you. Did Lucille have any other special friends I should talk to?"

"You been down to St. Francis?"

I nodded.

"You probably met all her friends then. She had friends from the old days, but she didn't go see them much. Of course, being elderly like she was, lots of her friends had already passed."

"Do you have any idea why someone would want to kill your cousin?"

She shook her head again. "It doesn't make a bit of sense to me. She was just a harmless old lady. She was real sweet-tempered. Sweeter than Betty, who really had a tongue in her head. Who would want to kill her?"

"Do you think she could have had anything that someone would kill her to get?"

"I thought about that. But what could it be? She was always broke. I can't see somebody killing her for thirty dollars' worth of food stamps. Then I thought, since Betty was killed, and Lucille was so nervous, maybe she had something of Betty's."

"That's what I've been thinking. But what?"

"I can't even come up with anything likely. It would have to be something she could carry around with her, like a will or an insurance policy or a piece of jewelry or something."

"Or a birth certificate or marriage license or a pack of letters for blackmail or a kilo of cocaine."

"Oh, Cousin Lucille wouldn't be caught dead with drugs."

She drew up short and caught her breath. "I mean — well, you know what I mean. She was raised Southern Baptist and she was Baptist all her life, even if she didn't go to church much these past few years. I think it was because she couldn't get all dressed up the way she was used to, and so for her last birthday I gave her a hat. Do you know she never wore it? She told me it was so nice she was saving it!

"Well, I didn't mean to get off track, but she thought drugs were Satan's props, and she wouldn't have anything to do with them."

"What can you tell me about your cousin's background? I'd like to know more about her."

"Well, I hate to admit how little I knew about her, when it comes right down to it. See, the family was from Georgia — that's where I grew up. Lucille's folks had moved north a while back, that's all I knew, so I only saw her maybe three times in my life before I moved here eight years ago. Lucille was my grandmother's sister's daughter. Her daddy worked in one of the meat packing houses here, but there was a story in the family about how he'd been an actor when he was a young man. Lucille was an actress, too, in her younger days. She even went to Hollywood and played in some movies. At least, that's what I heard from my mother, but when I asked Lucille about it, she wouldn't say, one way or the other. I never saw any movie she was in, but then, they would've been silents, and who sees those anymore? Anyway, I expect it was just a family legend.

"Her mother worked at the playing card company on the cleaning crew, and Lucille said she'd worked there, too. At some point, she married Cousin James, who worked in the same house her father worked in. I saw a picture of him once, and he was very handsome. But then, Lucille was always a striking woman — I don't know if you've seen a picture of her."

I shook my head, and she leaned over and pulled out a cabinet drawer. She handed me three photographs. One was an old black-and-white of a handsome Black woman in a print dress with shoulder pads and a hat. Her hair had been straightened and combed back from her face in one of those styles popularized by Veronica Lake when women went to work in the defense plants in the forties. I'd had one of those hairdos myself. Her head was thrown back and she was laughing. In the second one she was older, but she still looked young. It was another black-and-white, maybe from the late fifties, and she was wearing a suit and looking serious, sitting behind a table at a restaurant somewhere. The third was a color photo of the same woman, standing on the steps of this building. She was wearing a faded straight shirtwaist, a baggy sweater, socks, sneakers, and a knit hat. You could see wisps of gray hair sticking out from under the hat. She looked gaunt, weathered, sad. But Sophronia was right. She was still a striking woman.

"What happened to her husband?"

"It's a pretty sad story. Something went wrong with his arm — it was some kind of condition that men got who worked on the killing floor. I don't know if it was arthritis exactly, but I guess his shoulder hurt pretty bad and his hand became almost paralyzed. That was in the late thirties, and I guess he got some government compensation, but he didn't get anything from the company in those days. So Lucille went back to work, I think cleaning offices downtown. But I guess James got hard to live with once he was unemployed. She didn't talk about it, but I heard in the family that he was drinking a lot. Then James got cancer, and after a while she had to give up her job to stay home and take care of him. I think the family sent them money then, but you know how it is — hard enough to get by when somebody's working and everybody's healthy. And times were hard for everybody. Well, he died in the early fifties and we didn't hear much from Lucille after that. I don't really know what she lived on. She never told me. By the time I moved here, she was living on the streets, though it took me a while to figure that out."

"How did you find her?"

"My mother had an address from a Christmas card that was maybe two years old. It was an apartment building down on Findlay, but she didn't live there anymore. The manager said she still came by sometimes to visit, and so this lady gave Lucille my address the next time she came by and Lucille came around here. Like I say, it took me a while to catch on that she didn't have a place to live. But she was a proud woman and said to let her be. So I did. She always knew we were here if she needed us." A tear slipped down Sophronia's face, and we both ignored it.

I thought for a minute and realized I'd run out of questions. I thanked her and asked if I could contact her again if I thought of something.

"Of course. I wish you would. I mean, I know the police aren't going to run themselves ragged over the likes of Lucille Shelton. But somebody ought to be looking into those murders. Somebody ought to care about those two old ladies."

Hell, I was an old lady myself. As Kevin said, this case had my name written all over it.

CHAPTER 8

I decided it was time I met Bill McGann, impassioned leader of Street People United. Not that I figured him for a prime suspect; I didn't. But maybe he could tell me something about Betty that I didn't already know.

He sounded friendly on the phone but said he was about to leave town for two days — some agitators' convention in Chicago. In my mind's eye I saw workshops in confrontation techniques, optimizing the sit-in situation, and ripping off city resources. He agreed to see me on Saturday.

At nine o'clock, Eddie Landau called me. There was a cash register ringing in the background. I figured he was at Skyline Chili, checking out the drug scene under cover of a five-way.

"I thought you'd like to know that we struck gold on that Shelton PM," he said.

"It's about time. What'd you find?"

"It was lodged in the back of her throat, like part-way down her esophagus: a key to a safe deposit box."

"No shit! Have you tracked it down?"

"Not yet. We should have it traced by the end of the day tomorrow. I'll call as soon as I hear anything. But remember, you're not getting any of this from me."

"Me who?" I said, and hung up the phone.

I spent the next day at The Beach water park with Mabel, an excursion that would show up on my tax returns as a field study of human psychology. True to his word, Eddie called that night a little after seven. I was balancing a gin and tonic on my sunburned forehead and Mel was rubbing me down with aloe vera lotion.

The key belonged to a safe deposit box at Fifth Third Bank downtown. The box belonged to an Elizabeth Fay Grumbacher. Both Elizabeth and her mother had had accounts at the bank for some years, but the mother had died about twenty years ago, and Elizabeth had closed her account ten years ago. The box contained two things. The first was a batch of clippings from some newspapers from the twenties, all about a silent film star named Leda Marrs. The second was a will, dated from last year, in which Elizabeth Fay Grumbacher left all of her property to her daughter, Helen Jewett Prescott, of Clermont County, Ohio. The executrix of the estate was to be Lucille Eleanor Thornbush Shelton.

CHAPTER 9

What the hell did that mean, "all her property"? If there was one thing I didn't associate with Betty Bags, it was property. But the damn will was recent. Did she mean to leave her daughter the contents of four shopping bags, or did she have an Italian villa up her sleeve? That's assuming, of course, that Elizabeth Grumbacher and Betty Bags were one and the same.

And what about the Leda Marrs clippings? Had Betty Grumbacher once been president of the Cincinnati chapter of the Leda Marrs fan club? I remembered the name vaguely, though Marrs hadn't survived the silent era, and I didn't think I'd seen one of her movies. I knew that women supposedly killed themselves when Valentino died, and I supposed that the female movie stars had enjoyed their own following. Lucille Shelton had been to Hollywood, according to her cousin. Maybe these were Lucille's clippings, and Betty was letting her use the safe deposit box to store them. Maybe she used to work with Marrs and brought these back to show people how near to fame she'd been. I didn't know much about movies before my time, but you didn't have to be a genius to figure out that the closest most Black actresses came to fame was to play the maid of a famous white actress.

And who'd drawn up the will? There was no attorney's name mentioned, according to Eddie, but there were three witnesses, with names and addresses. He said he wouldn't tell me what they were until the cops had talked to these people. Stingy bastard.

The next morning I trotted down to the courthouse with a list of questions. After four hours and a cheese coney from a hot dog stand outside, I had some answers. Edgar P. Kirkendahl had never owned the Catatonia Arms. Nor did he own Sophronia Hewlett's building, which I thought I'd check on for good measure. Elizabeth Fay Grumbacher had been born on June 11, 1905, to Mildred Frances Hochs Grumbacher and Reginald August Grumbacher. That made her seventy-nine — not bad for a life on the streets. The dusty, washed-out blonde who was helping me couldn't come up with a marriage record for Betty, which struck me as odd. Not once in seventy-nine years? The woman had been a tower of resistance. In my day and before, you'd have had to work hard to escape being married. Maybe she'd been a bluestocking, a free spirit. Or maybe she'd just had the hots for Leda Marrs.

When Dusty brought me the probate records, I could barely restrain my glee. With my reading glasses perched on my nose, dust smudges on my cheeks, and a pen stuck behind my ear, I looked like the nightmare version of Donna Reed in *It's a Wonderful Life*, or like the pre-psychoanalysis Bette Davis in *Now, Voyager*. But I felt like Greer Garson discovering radium. According to the record, the attorney who had handled the Mildred Frances Hochs Grumbacher estate was named Harold Waite. I hoped to hell he hadn't kicked the bucket since.

I nipped down to the pay phone and let my fingers do the walking. There he was: Harold Waite, atty., in the Carew Tower. To be on the safe side, I called Homicide first. Eddie was out, Fricke was in. Just my luck. Fricke wouldn't give me the time of day, not willingly, so I had to outsmart him. This was not a challenge. He wouldn't tell me whether they'd tracked down the attorney who'd made the will. He wouldn't tell me if they'd talked to the three witnesses. He popped his gum in my ear and suggested I leave the investigation to the experts. I refrained from pointing out that Joe Friday never chewed gum and I hadn't met any experts. At least, I said in mock sympathy, they'd identified Betty's next of kin. That's how I got him to tell me what I really wanted to know: Helen Prescott said she'd never heard of an Elizabeth Fay Grumbacher.

Waite answered the phone himself, which surprised me.

He seemed taken aback that anyone wanted to talk about Betty Grumbacher, and he handed me the Hippocratic Oath that lawyers give out about client confidentiality. I told him his client was dead. He asked me to come see him at two-thirty.

I was right, he said, after I'd tripped over the Berber carpet in his waiting room and whanged my elbow on some goddamn Oriental antique: Betty Grumbacher was dead. He'd checked with the police. I bit my tongue, rubbed my arm, and followed him into an office with a wide-screen view of the river and Kentucky beyond.

Harold Waite was medium tall for a man, well within the range of a "little bit" shorter than Leon Jakes, with sandy hair liberally streaked with gray. He was tan and athletic-looking. He might have been Betty's age, or twenty years younger; it was hard to tell. I pegged him as the type with a charter membership in some hot-shit CEO health club, the kind with racquetball courts and wall-to-wall tanning booths. I was instantly suspicious.

He explained to me that he was semi-retired, with a summer home on the ninth fairway in the Woodlands and a winter home in Florida. I'd been lucky to catch him. He was usually in Florida by now. My suspicions multiplied.

"How long had you known Betty?"

"Forever." He flashed me a set of teeth that his dentist must be proud of. "We go way back, Betty and me. We grew up together on the West Side. I even dated Betty for a time in high school. She was a good looker in those days — before the booze and the pills and the hard luck. I even thought about marrying her. Then Billy came along — love's old sweet song, and all that." He chuckled. "Seems funny now to think back on all that."

"Who's Billy?"

"Oh, Billy. Yes, I forgot you wouldn't know who he was. Bill Buckner, Betty's first husband."

"I couldn't find a marriage certificate at the courthouse."

"No, you wouldn't. They ran off someplace to get hitched. Was it Louisville? She was on the young side, and Mildred would never have approved. As a matter of fact, Mildred had a cat when she found out." He laughed again.

"What happened then?"

"Oh, the usual thing, I guess. Two kids too young to be married. A nagging mother-in-law. The pressure."

"You said he was her *first* husband. Was Helen Jewett Prescott his daughter?"

"No, they didn't have kids. Helen came later. She was the only one, as far as I know, and even though Betty gave her up for adoption, she adored that kid — if you can call it that, since she hadn't seen the daughter since she was a baby. In fact, I drew up that will free of charge, as a favor to Betty. She acted like she didn't have much money, and she wanted to save what she had for Helen, though I got mixed messages about how much money she did have. Well, that's what she said, and who am I to argue with a lady?"

I didn't answer that one. He hadn't financed that outer office doing charity work.

"What makes you think she had money? You knew she was living on the streets, didn't you?"

"Well, let's just say I had my reasons. And I must have been right, too, because a few months back she came to see me about arranging an anonymous donation to some screwball charity she was interested in."

I was way ahead of him. "Street People United?"

"That's the one. She brought me a cashier's check for a thousand dollars, told me to take out a hundred and pass the rest on to this charlatan, Bill McGann. I tried to talk her out of it. 'If you've got money, Betty,' I said, 'why don't you let me invest it for you? You can't just let money sit around these days. You should be investing it, for Helen's sake. And you damn for sure shouldn't be throwing it away on some cockamamie organization.' 'Don't you worry, Harry,' she said. 'There's money left for Helen. And it's well invested, too.'"

"Did she tell you how she'd invested it?"

"No, not a word. I just hoped she hadn't handed it over to some con man, like one of those pals of hers."

"Did you know her pals?"

He looked at me like I'd just asked him if he'd ever dated Tokyo Rose.

"Did you ever hear about a run-in she'd had a while back with Edgar P. Kirkendahl?" I asked.

"Who, Betty?"

"Yes."

"No. What about?"

"She participated in an SPU demonstration at one of Kirkendahl's abandoned buildings. I believe she was arrested."

"Arrested? Betty? I can't understand why she never told me. For that matter, how did her bail get paid? I wonder who she called if she didn't call me." He thought a minute. "No, I didn't know anything about it. But if I had, I would have advised her not to tangle with Kirkendahl. He's out of her league."

"Why do you say that?"

"Well, it's obvious, isn't it? He's one of the most well-connected, powerful men in the city. He's not one to stand still for a bunch of tramps taking over his buildings and destroying his property. If it had come to that, I would have thanked my lucky stars that she hadn't called me. My best hope, frankly, would be appeasement, and if that didn't work, I'd hope to appeal to the jury's sympathy for an elderly woman with a history of mental illness."

"*Did* she have a history of mental illness?"

"Oh, yes. Betty was in and out of the hospital more times than I can count. That's how she ran through her mother's inheritance. And it's probably why she ended up on the streets. She had friends, you know, or at least her mother did. And none of us wanted her living like that. But she was damned stubborn, and as I say, she had a screw loose somewhere."

"But I don't get it, Mr. Waite. She said she had money, and she once gave you a thousand dollars."

"Gave it to Street People United, you mean."

"Right. Gave it to SPU. But if she had no obvious source of income, and she'd spent her inheritance, and had mental problems to boot, what made you think there was more where that came from?"

He looked at me a moment.

"I beg your pardon. I thought you knew. Betty Grumbacher was Leda Marrs."

CHAPTER 10

You know that feeling you get sometimes that you know what someone is going to say just before they say it? I had that feeling then, and still, I was shocked. Don't ask me why.

Why didn't I think Betty Grumbacher had once had a life worth living, even a life of fame and fortune? People end up on the streets. Mostly, they don't start out there. And old movie stars don't all end up in decaying mansions on Sunset Boulevard like Gloria Swanson. Some of them probably sell insurance in Poughkeepsie, or real estate in Orlando, or radio advertising in Des Moines. And some of them hit the skids and get put out of commission permanently, like Betty Grumbacher and just about every Black actress I could think of, maybe including Lucille Thornbush Shelton. They die in cities and towns all over America, without enough money to pay for a funeral. Sometimes you hear about it and sometimes you don't. One night, you see them on the late, late show, and think, "I wonder what ever happened to what's-her-face?" I didn't have to wonder any more about Leda Marrs, except for the part in between.

Maybe you remember her. I honest-to-God couldn't connect her face with the one on the corpse I'd seen, but I seemed to remember a dark-haired beauty, bow lips and eyes outlined in kohl. But maybe they all looked like that. I knew she was big. She was one of those smoldering vamp types, more Pola Negri than Mary Pickford or Lillian Gish, some production company's answer to Theda Bara after Bara's career was on the slide. Waite showed me an autographed photo, and it was just like I pictured, only she was laughing instead of smoldering. She was wearing a drop-waist beaded dress I would have killed for and a white fox somebody else had killed for. She was holding a champagne glass in one hand and a cigarette holder in the other. Across the corner was written, "All the best — hugs and kisses to Harry — Betty."

"Her mother was the ambitious one," Waite said. "Mildred had been a dancer in New York, strictly chorus line. She had Betty signed up for dance lessons by the time she was five, then acting and voice. Of course, voice didn't mean much then in Hollywood — that was before talkies — but I guess Mildred had some idea of starting her in New York. That's one reason she was so het up about the marriage, thought it ruined her daughter's chance for a career. Fortunately, I suppose, it didn't last long, and Mildred decided to hustle Betty off to Hollywood, where people were beginning to make a fortune in motion pictures."

"Was there a Mr. Grumbacher?" The birth certificate had mentioned a Reginald August, which sounds like the kind of name somebody'd make up.

"He'd either died or disappeared when Betty was a kid. Mildred always spoke of him as 'my late husband,' but to tell you the truth, I was never sure how to take that."

"So Betty went to Hollywood. When was that?"

"I couldn't say for sure. I was several years out of high school, so it must have been in the late teens, just after the war — the first war, that is. Well, a few years went by, and suddenly little Betty Grumbacher, now known as Leda Marrs, had hit the big time. I remember the first movie of hers I saw — something about Christians hiding out in catacombs.

She was the evil seductress who betrayed the Christians to the Romans, but people apparently liked her. It was strange, seeing somebody you'd known all your life up there on the screen."

"Did she earn a lot of money?"

"Must have, at least when her career was at its height. Spent a lot, too, from what her mother told me. Mildred came back home after a few years — I never found out why. Left her daughter to her wild living, from what I gather. But by the end of the twenties, what with sound coming in and the crash and all, Betty couldn't keep it up. Well, I don't know the whole story, so I can't really say why her career went bust. But it did, and she came home to her mother, who by that time was having spells of sickness. Trouble was, Betty had them, too, only in Betty's case, it was depression — pills and booze and half-hearted suicide attempts. I saw less and less of them over the years. Oh, I took care of their legal affairs, such as they were, mostly Mildred's will. When Mildred died in 1962, I handled the probate. Betty seemed to have aged a lot over the years. You'd never have picked her for a famous movie star."

"Didn't she ever remarry?"

"Who, Betty? Not that I know of, but she might have. I wouldn't really know."

"But you said the daughter wasn't Billy's."

"Well, I confess that when she made that will, it came as quite a surprise to me, and I asked. She said the woman wasn't Billy's daughter, and she wouldn't tell me anything more about it."

"So what happened next?"

"Oh, I don't know. I couldn't even tell you when she ended up on the streets. If I'd known, I might have done something. Well, I could have had her committed once I found out, but they weren't doing that so much anymore, and anyway, she said she was happy and I should leave her alone. She was pretty forceful in her later years, so I stopped arguing with her. It was her life, not my place to tell her what to do."

"But you *did* try to tell her when she came to you with the money for SPU," I pointed out.

"Yes, well, I felt it was my duty as her attorney to advise her on the disposition of her estate. Not the same as proposing that she check into a mental hospital. It amounted to the same thing, I guess, since I felt fairly certain she'd lost all her marbles if she had this kind of money and was living on the streets, and especially if she was going to start giving it away."

"'Start'? Did you think there were more contributions to come?"

"Oh, I don't know that I meant that exactly, but I suppose I thought there might be. This McGann character strikes me as the unscrupulous type, stirring people up to see what he can get out of them. I thought he'd see her as a permanent meal ticket."

"But she made the contribution anonymously."

"Yes, she did. She was that careful, at least. Still, I didn't put it past him to find out somehow and go looking for more."

"And you thought there was more. Was that because of what she earned as an actress during her heyday?"

"If you mean her salary, that was only part of it. Don't you ever remember reading about the kind of presents movie stars received from their adoring fans and admirers? Cars, yachts, houses — hell, in the boom days of the twenties, a movie actress could expect to clear a fortune in gifts alone."

"What about jewelry?" I was thinking more along the lines of something that fit in a shopping bag.

"Sure, that, too. As a matter of fact, there *was* a famous piece of jewelry associated with Betty."

My ears twitched like the cats' when they hear the call of the can opener. "Yes?"

"It was something called the Velazquez emerald, named after the mine in Colombia where it was found. It was set in a necklace of pearls and diamonds, and the press went wild when it showed up dangling from Betty's neck. Some gossip columnist recognized it, and the rumors attributed it to an Arab sheik who was paying Betty a lot of attention in those days. I guess neither the sheik nor Betty confirmed it. Eventually, the sheik disappeared, and the necklace disappeared, and nobody knows where it went."

I thought a minute.

"Do you know the names of any of these boyfriends? The sheik and so on?"

"No, I don't. But tell you what you do. You go talk to the fellow at Xavier — he could tell you anything you want to know about Betty. He wrote a whole book about her, interviewed all kinds of people, even me. Now, what the hell was his name? I bought a copy of the book, but I'm afraid it's down in Florida."

"Do you remember the title?"

"Oh, it was something corny like *Golden Star* or *Rising Star* — something like that. I know it had 'star' in it somewhere."

"I'll ask Lucille Shelton. I bet she'd know." This was my attempt to catch him off guard, and I thought it was too clever for words. But if he recognized the name, he didn't show it.

"Who was that you said?"

"Lucille Shelton. Betty's best friend."

"Oh. I don't believe I've met her, though I recognize the name from Betty's will. She's the executrix, I think, so I suppose I'll be meeting with her soon. Like I said, I didn't know too many of Betty's friends."

I wasn't going to be the one to tell him that he'd never be meeting with Lucille. "Well," I said, standing up and giving him my own best imitation of a smile, "I appreciate all your help. You've been very generous with your time."

"Not at all. Let me know if there's anything else I can do. Betty's death has shaken me a great deal, you know. We were once very close."

With my hand on the door, I turned back.

"Oh, just one more thing." The Columbo technique. It always worked for him. "If Betty really did have a fortune socked away somewhere, it wasn't in the bank, either in an account or in her safe deposit box. Unless you think she carried it around in shopping bags, which I admit is a possibility, or unless she had another account at another bank, it had to have been squirreled away somewhere. Where do you think it is?"

"Ah," he said, looking profound. "That's the sixty-four-thousand-dollar question, isn't it?"

* * *

The public library was three blocks up Vine Street, so I decided to cruise by and see if I could find the "star" book. I looked up Marrs, Leda, in the card catalog, and there it was: *Morning Star: The Story of Leda Marrs,* by Stephen Grunewald. It had been published in 1973 — eleven years ago — so I hoped that Grunewald still taught at Xavier. Just for good measure, I looked up Shelton, Lucille. Not a goddamn thing.

I found Betty's book on the shelf in the film section. That meant the librarians expected it to be popular, so they hadn't shelved it in the stacks. I wondered if the librarians were right. Betty may have been a local celebrity of sorts, but she didn't seem to have made much money off of her fame in recent years.

I would have to take the book home and read it cover to cover, but I was too damn curious not to take a peek inside. I flipped to the plates. After the run-of-the-mill baby pictures came one in which Mildred, a proud mama with pins in her mouth, was working on Betty's image. Betty was dressed as a gypsy for Halloween, lipstick and all. She might have been nine or ten, and though she was smiling at the camera, she had an enigmatic air about her. In one hand she held a crystal ball, or a ball covered with aluminum foil, and she had her head cocked to one side, her other hand on her hip. She was getting into character.

After that came a sequence from her films. In the first, she was waiting tables in the background while a fight took place in the foreground; the caption told you where to find her. In the second, she was wearing an outlandish wraparound number, something like a cross between a tunic and a toga, carrying a torch and giving the camera a sultry look. The set looked like some kind of cave. According to the caption, this came from *The Beautiful Martyr*, the film that made Betty a star. Other pictures were stills from such films as *Dangerous Lady* (with co-star Francis X. Bushman), *Eve's Daughters*, *Cleopatra of Egypt*, and *Satan's Handmaiden* (with Valentino). You can probably imagine the costumes.

There were four other pictures, one a duplicate of Harry's, which must have been a publicity shot for the production company. In another, she had her hand draped over the arm of a handsome foreign guy, whom the caption identified as Sheik Ali Khabril. For once, she wasn't posing for the camera. In fact, she looked surprised and a little pissed off that someone was taking her picture. In the third, she was standing between Douglas Fairbanks and Tyrone Power, arms linked, laughing.

It was the fourth picture that most attracted my attention. It was a still from *The Temptress*. Betty was dressed in a slinky gown, lying stretched on a chaise lounge. Behind her, a woman dressed like a maid was putting her hair up. According to the caption, the maid was Lucille Shelton.

CHAPTER 11

"You're kidding! *Leda Marrs? The* Leda Marrs?" Kevin had just scored a direct hit on a bowl of corn flakes with the grapefruit he'd been holding. The combined effects of noise and fallout sent Sidney scrambling, little flakelets clinging to his fur.

"What do *you* know about Leda Marrs?" I said. "Her star had set long before your mother was born, almost before I was born, even."

"Well, so had Benedict Arnold's, and I know who he was. I'm not illiterate, for god's sake. I used to hang out at the Pantheon Theater on weekends, and I saw lots of old silents, sometimes with music and sometimes without. God, Leda Marrs was one of my favorites. And to think her body was lying right over my head, and I didn't even know it! It gives me the shivers."

He did look a little pale. He sat down.

"Leda Marrs," he said again, shaking his head sadly. "What a loss! When I think of how she looked right before she stabbed Tyrone Power in *What a Woman Can Do . . .*" He put down the knife he was planning to use on the grapefruit. "I mean, it's not as if she didn't have practice. He must have held a gun on her, like Wallace Beery did in Wages of *Sin*. Do you think that was it?"

"I think you're confusing art and life."

"Well," he said in an offended voice, "she *did* lead a life that came right out of a movie script. I read somewhere that she had three cars at one point, and a swimming pool in the shape of a heart, which she filled with champagne on her birthday. She once sold off a closetful of furs and gave the proceeds to the SPCA."

"Sounds like you read the same biography I'm reading."

"The one with the dumb title? Something about a star?"

"*Morning* Star, by Stephen Grunewald."

"That's the one. I read it when it came out."

"I'm only up to her first big movie, and already I'm dreading the rest because I know how it ends."

"Hey, I just thought of something! If Betty Grumbacher was Leda Marrs, maybe you can find this guy Grunewald, and call him on the phone, and see if he has any ideas about who killed her!"

"I can do better than that. He teaches at Xavier."

"Uh-oh."

"Why 'uh-oh'?"

He gave me a withering look. "Don't you see? Come on, Mrs. C, use your gray cells. If this biographer is a local, he should be on your list of suspects."

"I know he should be. That's why I'm going to see him."

"Maybe he found out something while he was researching the biography, and he was blackmailing her, and she finally threatened to go to the police. Maybe it has something to do with this daughter — the one who never heard of Betty. Maybe he knew who the father was."

"Maybe he was the father."

"I think you're confusing art and life, Mrs. C." His cornflakes had been reduced to dust, and he stirred them slowly. "Wasn't there some famous piece of jewelry she owned — some present she got from a prince or somebody?"

"An emerald necklace, the Velazquez emerald, to be exact. A present from Sheik Ali Khabril."

"Sheik, shit! That choker must be worth a fortune! Maybe she'd been carrying it around in a shopping bag all these years, and somebody knew it or found out about it, and killed her to get it. But if it's sold on the black market, how will we ever know?"

"I agree that they wanted something from her, and it may have been the necklace. But I don't think they got whatever it was they were after."

"Why not?"

"You're forgetting Lucille. I have a feeling Lucille got forgotten a lot in her life."

"Of course! Lucille! They went after Lucille! And Lucille had the key to Betty's safe deposit box. But there wasn't anything in the box except for the will and those clippings."

"And Lucille's body was nude, so I suspect they searched her clothing."

"Which means they were looking for something small, or at least portable. Like an emerald necklace or a key to a safe deposit box."

"And Lucille at least thought that the key was valuable, because she swallowed it."

"That's right! So either she didn't know that what was in the box wasn't valuable, or—"

"What was in the box *was* valuable, and the cops didn't realize it."

"Mrs. C! What if the clippings are marked in some kind of code — like the early Christians used in *The Beautiful Martyr.*"

"I never heard of early Christians using code."

"So, they borrowed it from Conan Doyle. Don't be such a critic! The question is whether Betty borrowed it from *The Beautiful Martyr.*"

"I don't know. Sounds far-fetched to me."

"Mrs. C, I'm surprised at you! If you don't use your imagination, you'll never make a great detective! Name me one thing that's happened in this case so far that *isn't* far-fetched."

"Starting with the part about the murdered bag lady showing up in Number Three at the Catatonia Arms and then turning out to be a famous silent film star? Okay, I'll grant you things have been a bit strange."

"I'm telling you, Mrs. C. Anybody who's lived in Hollywood and been involved with movies for any length of time at all comes away with their head screwed on funny. I know about these things. I'm a bartender. And that includes anyone who donated her drawers to the Smithsonian."

"She didn't!"

"Haven't you gotten to that part yet? Of course, she did. And the Smithsonian threw a big party to celebrate."

"Well, in any case, I have to figure out how to get my mitts on the contents of that damned safe deposit box."

"Do you think you can?"

"I don't know. But if I do, I ought to get double points towards my P.I. license."

"Yeah," he said thoughtfully, missing his cup and pouring coffee on top of the cornflake crumbs.

"Listen, Mr. Know-It-All. If you saw all of Betty's films, you must have seen the ones with Lucille Shelton, or Lucille Thornbush, as she was then. One of them was called *The Temptress.*"

"Was that Tyrone Power, too?"

"Yes, and it sounds to me like a rehash of *Blood and Sand*, except the man's a prizefighter instead of a bullfighter, and it takes place in New York instead of Spain."

"I do remember it, kind of. I can't say that I remember much about Lucille's role, though."

"You're not supposed to. She played the maid. Also in *Dangerous Lady* and *Wages of Sin*. There might have been others; those are the only ones he mentions."

"Did you look her up in anything?"

"Yeah, I checked a couple of film encyclopedias. She only showed up in one out of the four I looked at, and her entry was about three lines long."

"Did it tell you anything about her life?"

"Yeah, where she was born, what her major films were, and when she left Hollywood."

"Three lines! Imagine a life summed up in three lines. Depressing, isn't it? And Betty, too. Now that I know she was Leda Marrs, it all makes sense to me. Just like Clara Bow."

"What about Clara Bow?"

"Oh, you know, she had such a tragic life after she left movies — during, too, I guess. She couldn't make it in sound pictures because of her Brooklyn accent. She had a whole series of nervous breakdowns and died in a sanitarium somewhere in the sixties. Who knows what happens to women like that? Even while they're successful, they have to start worrying about what will happen when it all goes away — like when somebody decides they're too old to play romantic leads. Men never seem to get too old to play romantic leads. Look at John Wayne. Look at Cary Grant. But women in their mid-twenties are over the hill in Hollywood. They only get to play psychopaths, like Joan Crawford and Bette Davis."

"Yeah, and we make it possible, for chrissake, the way we worship the goddamn picture of perfection that Hollywood gives us. I mean, am I disgusted when I see Jean Harlow in *Dinner at Eight* wearing a dress she can't sit down in? Do I look at that dress and think 'permanent kidney damage'? Hell, no! I watch her and think how nice it would be to be that skinny, and then I wonder if blondes really do have more fun. Shit like that. And if most white women don't measure up, then Black women sure as hell can't."

"You're right, Mrs. C. We helped put Betty and Lucille on the streets if it comes to that."

"But we're not going to let the bastard that killed them get away with murder."

* * *

So that night I finished Betty's biography, sitting up in bed with a fan on my face and a pina colada on the nightstand. It was all there: the golden years, with a string of famous men at her beck and call, the heavy drinking and late nights, the slow unraveling of the fabric that Mildred had woven so carefully, the rumors that Leda Marrs was "difficult," inattentive, not as young as she used to be (at twenty-six!), the famous eleven-month "disappearance," during which her agent said she was resting, the gradual decline in offers, and finally the return in defeat, mansions, cars, and furs all sold to pay debts. As if to indicate that her life effectively ended when she departed the public eye, Grunewald covered the next three decades in two chapters, the last one more eulogy than biography. He left her sitting alone in a shabby one-room apartment, surrounded by the dregs of her life, doomed to return again and again to the state mental hospital.

Well, to tell you the truth, this last chapter changed my perspective. Grunewald made it sound as if death was the best thing that could happen to her. But somehow she'd worked up the spunk and energy to move on, was how I saw it. And even if she'd moved on to the streets, I began to see that as a preferable alternative to sitting on her ass in a one-room apartment. Street people have to work hard to survive. Like my pals at St. Francis pointed out, Betty had her territory to cover every day, and every day she hit the streets and made a living out of whatever she could dig out of trash cans and dumpsters and discarded crates. And in the final months of her life, she'd become committed to the cause of helping her own kind.

And what about Lucille? Grunewald had obviously talked to her, but he'd been interested in Betty's story, not Lucille's. I learned that they'd met in dance class in Cincinnati as kids but didn't know each other well until they both ended up in Hollywood at the same time. According to Grunewald, Lucille paid Betty numerous compliments, but they were of the vapid, cliché-ridden kind that made me suspect Grunewald of inventing half of them. You know how sometimes people hear what they want to hear? That's how it struck me, anyway.

Nothing about how Lucille's fortunes declined. Nothing to suggest that they were now more than casual friends.

Nothing about what happened to the famous emerald necklace. Nothing about whether Betty was tracking her adopted daughter. Nothing to explain why Betty and Lucille had been murdered on the streets of Cincinnati.

I studied the face on the back inside flap of the book jacket.

Stephen Grunewald looked like a nice man — round face, short curly hair, glasses — but I knew better than to trust his looks. He was probably in actuality a son of a bitch, with a terrible temper, gambling debts, and an ex-wife who hated his guts. And he might, just possibly, be a murderer.

Looking at his picture gave me an idea. The next morning, I steered the bomber down to the library again and picked up a few things. I found a picture of Harry Waite in a Cincinnati Bar Association book. It came as no surprise to me that he had once been treasurer three years running. McGann wasn't so easy, though, since the most obvious pictures were the ones in the newspaper, and you can't check those out. But I read up on him in the newspapers and found out he was a U.C. grad, School of Planning. Sure enough, he'd done me the favor of getting his mug in the yearbook — a gaunt face with those creases in his jaw like Jason Robards, longish dark hair and sideburns. None of this was ideal, of course, since all of these photographs were old, and people can change a lot over time, especially when they have a reason to disguise their appearance. But it gave me a lineup of sorts.

I found Leon painting the storeroom in the back of La Pooch, the T-shirt design store. He was going at it with the seriousness of a great artist, designing his own T-shirt and jeans as he went along. First, he'd work his roller around in the paint a while, till he had it saturated with half a can of the stuff. Then he held it waist-high, dribbling paint all over his sneakers and drop cloth, while he contemplated his next stroke. And finally, with a mathematician's precision, he applied it to the wall in one long sweeping motion, approximately an inch to the left of the last stroke.

The guy who took me back to see him laughed at the expression on my face.

"Ahh, don't worry, he fills it all in eventually. I don't give him no advice. Hell, he's a professional like me. Plus, he's got a passion for paint. He takes half of it home with him, but what do I care? I like to see a man happy in his work, know what I mean?"

I broke into Leon's concentration and motioned him over, suggesting that he leave the paint roller behind. "Hey, Leon, it's Cat. Remember me?"

"Uh-huh, yes'm, Miz Cat, I remember."

I let the "Miss" go to save my breath.

"Good. Do you remember when I asked you about the man and woman you saw that day when you were sweeping in front of Cecil's? And you said you'd know the man again if you saw him?"

"Uh-huh." He nodded once, and blinked for emphasis. I laid out my three pictures — Grunewald, Waite, and McGann.

"I want you to look at these three men. Take your time, now, and study their faces." He studied. "Do any of them look familiar?"

"Uh-huh."

"They do?" My heart rushed up to greet my tonsils. "Which one?"

"This here one." He fingered Waite.

"He look k-kind of like my Uncle Jerome 'f-fore he growed his mustache."

Damned if I wasn't playing straight woman to a stand-up comic.

CHAPTER 12

Now that I'd read Betty's biography and all, I was more interested in the Hollywood angle than any other possible theories about her murder. Who wouldn't be? I had visions of a spread in *People* magazine at the very least, maybe a film script. I know it sounds crass, even insensitive, no doubt morally reprehensible, and I made every effort to squelch such thoughts. But they crept in anyway, like little mice do when they find the tiniest crack in the wall and invite all their friends in for a party in your pantry.

Nevertheless, we detectives are trained to follow up every lead. And since I had an appointment with Bill McGann, I resolutely turned my back on my pet theory and headed off to interview McGann with all the enthusiasm of Rosalind Russell in *His Girl Friday*. But without the hat.

It was one of those airless summer days when the weather forecasters were talking heat inversion, and Cincinnati smelled like a mixture of soap from the Procter & Gamble plant and whiskey from the Canadian distillery. I was wearing a respectable white skirt, a Bonnie Raitt T-shirt that Franny had given me for Mother's Day and a pair of sandals that squeaked from the sweat when I walked. The key here, I thought, was to avoid intimidating McGann. I left my shoulder holster at home.

Street People United had an office over a storefront on West 4th in a building that looked like it might be condemned any day the inspectors noticed it. I figured the owner got away with a lot because between the junk stores, which sold junk, and the art galleries, which sold art that often resembled junk, it was sort of hard to tell what was what.

A garish sign done in fuchsia and lime green proclaimed the location of the SPU office from a second-floor window. I took the stairs. The elevator was one of those rickety jobs with the folding grate of black metal — probably made by a company that went out of business in the thirties. A spider regarded me from its web, which was draped across one corner of the door to SPU. Inside I could hear the slow, erratic clacking of manual typewriter keys.

The office consisted of one large room that reminded me of some campaign headquarters I'd seen — desks arranged haphazardly, crap piled all over the place, a broken-down sofa wedged into one corner, file drawers standing open. The mad typist turned out to be none other than Bill McGann himself. He didn't look anything like his yearbook picture. He was short, maybe a foot taller than me, which meant he *could* have corresponded to Leon's idea of "not too tall," depending on what Leon meant by a "little bit" shorter than he was. McGann had brown wavy hair and a bald spot. He was wearing glasses held together at one corner by about a yard of electrician's tape. He also wore faded jeans, a Greenpeace Save the Whales T-shirt, and a pair of Birkenstocks. The sixties live.

He cleared a space for me on a chair and a space for himself to perch on a nearby desk. A fan in the corner ground away with all the effect of an elf trying to blow out a bonfire. Bill and I took turns dripping on his threadbare mud-colored carpet.

"Yeah, the guys told me to expect you, so I wasn't surprised when you called. It's good to see *somebody* taking some action. Goddamn cops couldn't care less, of course. Did you get one of our flyers?"

He handed me a bad mimeograph on pink paper. It announced a candlelight vigil on Fountain Square Sunday night, in memory of Betty and Lucille. There was also some stuff, printed in all caps, about the cops not taking the murders seriously. If Fricke had seen it, my guess was he'd turned the same color as the flyer.

"Thanks," I said. "I'll plan to be there. Meanwhile, I'd like to hear something from you about Betty's involvement with SPU."

"Sure. Glad to help any way I can. Let's see. Betty came to her first meeting, oh, maybe six months back. Curtis Lamont brought her and her friend Lucille. She was kind of a tough customer, Betty. You know the type. Nothing would work, the world was against us, nobody would ever listen to us, nothing would ever change. We're used to that." He had the politician's trick of always speaking in the first person plural — a habit that tends to arouse my suspicion. "But we brought her around eventually, and once she converted, there was no stopping her. She took to dropping by a few times a week, helping me with office work or just shooting the breeze. She had some good ideas about organizing, too." He laughed suddenly and shook his head. "Of course, I'm not saying she was our best recruiter. Once she was sold on the idea of SPU, she didn't have a hell of a lot of patience for people who didn't see things her way. I tried to tell her that you couldn't bully people into becoming committed to a cause, but I think it went in one ear and out the other. Luckily, most people took Betty with a grain of salt and didn't hold her against us." He looked at me to make sure I was following.

"Don't get me wrong. I loved Betty. I got along well with her, and I admired her for not taking any shit from anybody. She gave this organization a lot of energy."

"And what about Lucille? Did she get involved, too?"

"Oh, sure. Not as involved as Betty, but then she had some family around, I think. She wasn't as outgoing as Betty was, either. She was kind of quiet. But I'll tell you something, she didn't take as much persuading as Betty did in the beginning. Maybe because it didn't take much to convince her that oppressed people needed to band together in order to force change. See, Betty didn't have that perspective, and I think Lucille probably, in her own quiet way, made Betty understand the importance of our work. So sometimes when Betty came by to work in the office, she brought Lucille, and sometimes she came by herself."

"Did you ever hear Betty talk about her family when she was sitting around 'shooting the breeze,' as you call it?"

"You know, it's interesting you ask that. I remember once she got to talking about her mother, and how much her mother wanted her to succeed in life. I remember that, because she said something about how well she'd started out, but she just couldn't keep it up. Well, I always find it interesting, where people come from and all. Every person out on the streets has a story. So I asked Betty what she'd done, just out of curiosity, you know, but she wouldn't say — just said it was too long ago to remember. And she told me she didn't have any sisters and brothers."

"Children?" I made this sound casual.

"No, no children, at least that I know of. But I remember we kind of talked about it once, just a month or so ago. See, my wife and I are trying to have a baby right now, and I mentioned it to Betty, and she seemed interested. Seemed sort of concerned, too, that I shouldn't be working here if I was going to be a father. I mean, right now I drive a cab part-time, and Mona — that's my wife — she works, too. So I don't depend on SPU for my income, though I pick up some salary off of grants. Well, I admit I don't make a lot of money, but we don't need a lot. She said it would be different when the baby came. And maybe she was right, but I wasn't willing to give up SPU just when things were getting going with it. And now, with Betty and Lucille murdered, I have even more reason to stick around."

"Do you have any ideas about who murdered them?"

"I wish I did. I know who I think is a big enough bastard to do it, but I don't know how to pin it on him."

"Are you referring to Edgar Kirkendahl?"

"Bingo. See, Betty hated his guts. Maybe that was my fault, because I hated his guts. I used to talk about some of the scams he'd pulled. He's the kind of son of a bitch who'd foreclose on his own grandmother if he saw a chance to turn a profit. 'So, Bill,' she'd say, 'why can't we get the goods on him? If he's the sleazeball you say he is, surely we can get something on him and then negotiate for a couple of shelters?' Well, I don't like to operate that way, to tell you the truth. I didn't want to sink to his level, and I said so. That's assuming, of course, that we ever could 'get the goods on him,' as she put it. He's such a slimy bastard, with so many people in his pocket, I doubt we'd ever come up with anything, and we might die trying."

I guess my ears quivered, because he nodded.

"Oh, sure, that's occurred to me, don't think it hasn't. She always said I was too naive and that I ought to fight Kirkendahl with the gloves off, because that was the only way he understood. She could be secretive, Betty could, and I think she enjoyed thinking of herself involved in some kind of cloak-and-dagger drama, so when she turned up murdered, I wondered if she'd gotten into something over her head."

"How might she have gone about 'getting the goods' on Kirkendahl, though? Did she say?"

"Not exactly. She did say once that now she'd been in jail for trespassing, she didn't have any qualms about going to jail for breaking and entering. And another time she said that there was one advantage to being a bag lady — people didn't look at you too closely. I guess I considered the possibility that she could've gone to Kirkendahl's office and pretended to be on the janitorial staff."

"You said she was really into this cloak-and-dagger stuff. Do you think she would have been good at it? I mean, would she have been able to pull it off?"

"Sure, why not? It's like she said — people don't really look at bag ladies, and they get lots of practice at being invisible. That's what SPU is all about, you know — making street people visible."

I saw that he'd jumped the track to land on his favorite topic, so I scrambled to intercept him.

"So you think she might have found something on Kirkendahl and then tried to negotiate a deal by herself?"

"Oh, that's one possibility, I guess. Or else Kirkendahl found out somehow that she knew something. I guess I think that's more likely. Secretive as she could be, I don't see how she could have kept something like that from me, or at least not for very long."

"But maybe it wasn't for very long, right? We don't have any way of knowing."

"Sure, that's true, too."

"How did you feel about the nine hundred dollars she gave you?" I ambushed him and got a suitably perplexed response.

"Nine hundred dollars? What nine hundred dollars?"

"Didn't you receive a nine hundred-dollar gift a while back?"

"The only one we received was anonymous, came through some hotshot lawyer's office. That wouldn't have had anything to do with Betty." He spoke with conviction.

"Why don't you think so?"

He shrugged. "Because it wouldn't, that's all. Betty didn't have that kind of money."

"How do you know?"

He was staring at me now.

"Because. Well, just because. If she had that kind of money, she wouldn't have been on the streets."

"But she *did* have that kind of money, and she told her lawyer, Harold Waite, that there was more where that came from, and that she was saving it for her daughter."

He stood up and walked to the window. He looked out through the strip of glass not covered by the cardboard sign.

"I can't believe it," he said slowly. "That's the right attorney, though — Graft, Graft, Feinstein and Waite. Nine hundred dollars from Betty. I'm stunned. I mean, some of the street people are eccentric, there's no doubt about it. Some of them have been institutionalized, and I knew Betty had. It's easy to oversimplify their reasons for being on the street, and of course it's to our advantage to emphasize the lack of affordable housing, jobs, and mental health care. But somehow I never think of any of them as benefactors to that extent. I mean, I figured some wealthy eccentric had read about us in the newspaper or seen us on TV and decided to help us out. I never guessed it was Betty. It never even crossed my mind."

Maybe he was protesting too much, but I didn't think so. It wouldn't have crossed my mind, either. I dropped my next bomb.

"Didn't you know that she had once been a silent film star named Leda Marrs?"

He turned around and looked at me, as if it didn't sink in at first. Then it registered.

"Leda Marrs? *Betty?*"

I nodded.

"You're not making this up, are you?"

I shook my head.

"You know, now that you mention it, I remember reading somewhere that Leda Marrs came from Cincinnati in some article on famous Cincinnatians. But *Betty?* I guess I should be embarrassed. Not that I didn't know, but that I find it so hard to believe now that I do know. After all, why shouldn't she be Leda Marrs?"

"I felt the same way," I confessed.

"Yeah, but you didn't *know* Betty. I don't suppose you ever saw her, except when she was dead. Not that I know much about Leda Marrs. I doubt if I've ever seen one of her movies. But still. The idea of Betty as a famous movie star is a shock. I feel like I should reassess everything I thought I knew about her, even though that's a stupid way to look at it. I mean, the person I knew was Betty. I never knew Leda Marrs."

"But you never had any inkling that Betty might have money?"

"No, of course not."

"She never showed you anything or said anything that made you wonder?" I was tiptoeing around in uncertain territory.

"No, why?"

"She never mentioned selling or pawning anything she owned to raise money?"

"No. What are you getting at?"

"She once owned a priceless emerald necklace, given to her in her youth by an Arab sheik. I don't suppose you ever saw anything like that."

His gaze traveled around the room as if he thought he might have walked through a mirror and ended up on the other side.

"No," he said finally.

"She never showed you any jewelry she might have owned?"

"The kind of stuff she showed me were knit hats, stray shoes, and half-empty bottles of nail polish. 'Look at this, Bill,' she'd say. 'Now why would somebody throw away a perfectly good purse like that? I can tape up that torn place and have me a purse that's good as new. People are so wasteful!' No, she never showed me an emerald necklace."

"Well, supposing — just supposing — that she owned an emerald necklace. And supposing she didn't want to carry it around with her in her shopping bags. And she wanted to put it away for safekeeping, and she didn't put it in her safe deposit box. And she wanted it somewhere where she could keep an eye on it, and know that it was safe, but wouldn't expect anybody else to find it. Where do you think she could put it?"

We looked at each other a minute, and then, in unison, our eyes shifted to the overstuffed file cabinet in the corner, crowded by boxes and picket signs, its drawers gaping to expose the untidy condition of their contents.

CHAPTER 13

I like to think of myself as a skeptical person. Suspicion is second nature to any woman who has raised three kids. But I admit that it's hard to be suspicious of a man you've played kneesies with, down on the floor by the filing cabinet.

"I guess I've gotta revamp my filing system," McGann said, extracting a bag of crushed potato chips from a folder labeled "Rents."

"Revamp?" I said. "Are you trying to tell me you *have* a filing system?" I was trying to pry apart two folders stuck together with an adhesive I suspected of being edible.

"Elvira Clark set it up." He nodded. "It's based on a modified shopping bag system."

"Oh," I said. "That explains it."

A Black man in a wheelchair appeared at the door. "Phone for you, Bill."

"Thanks." He stood up, brushing assorted crumbs from his pants. To me he said, "We don't have the money for a phone, so the veterans' group down the hall lets us use theirs. I'll be back."

When I heard his footsteps fade, I hunted around until I found a folder I'd spotted earlier: Kirkendahl and Associates. Inside was a bunch of clippings about Kirkendahl and his properties, mostly from the newspaper but some from a newsletter of some kind, maybe an SPU publication from the tone of it. Kirkendahl was charged with owning at least ten vacant buildings downtown, in addition to twelve others in disrepair, although he managed to collect exorbitant rents for the apartments in them. One newspaper article reported SPU accusations that Kirkendahl's buildings could only pass inspection if money was changing hands.

Kirkendahl denied these allegations in eloquent prose and elegant attire. He intimated that it was hardly worth his while to prosecute for slander at this time. Which meant he was leaving the door open. I wondered whether his stated reason was credible. A bastard of a slumlord like Kirkendahl must have a lawyer or two on retainer. Why not prosecute the SPU out of existence? I didn't believe for a minute that he couldn't buy a favorable decision, one way or another. Was he afraid of setting up the SPU for martyrdom?

Anyway, what did all this have to do with Betty? Suppose she had something on Kirkendahl. But it still didn't make sense. Betty was a nobody. How could she have anything on him that he couldn't buy his way out of? Of course, the fact that she was killed with her own knife suggested that the killing might not have been planned.

Maybe somebody was sent to collect documents from her and things got out of hand. Then after he killed her, he discovered that he still didn't have the documents. So he went after Lucille.

Taped to the inside cover of the folder was a piece of legal paper, folded to fit the folder size and covered with notes in a tiny, meticulous handwriting. It looked like a list of Kirkendahl-owned buildings and corresponding rents charged. I didn't see anything fishy there — at least, not at first. But it struck me as odd that the paper was taped in using masking tape, not cellophane tape like most offices used.

Of course, masking tape was probably cheaper and more in demand in an operation that depended upon posted notices to call attention to its activities. Still. I peeled off a length of tape and stuck it to the edge of the file drawer for safekeeping. My fingers explored the folded paper and extracted two more folded pieces of paper that looked like they'd been run over by a garbage truck (and maybe they had). They had the shine and texture of Xerox paper.

I heard a footstep in the hall and squelched my curiosity. I slipped the papers into my skirt pocket and taped the edges of the top sheet back down.

Also in the file were some notes in a handwriting that gave me a pain in the middle of my forehead. I turned my attention to them just as McGann loomed up behind me.

"Find anything?"

"No, I was just looking through your Kirkendahl file." I opted for the direct approach.

"Yeah? Anything useful?"

"What are these?"

"Oh," he said, scanning the top one. "This here's my grocery list." He crumpled it up and tossed it in the direction of the trash box. It hit the edge of a desk, ricocheted off the arm of a chair, skidded across a placard lying against the floor, and came to rest next to his shoe. He didn't notice. Next time I came, I expected to find it re-filed.

"Now this one is interesting." He scowled at it as if it were written by a stranger. It appeared to be written by a hyperactive four-year-old with dyslexia. "This is my note from our first phone conversation. Not my first call, you understand, since I'd called him twice a week for four months before I got to talk to him. But here's where I suggested he convert his building on Findlay to subsidized housing."

"Did he agree?"

"He said it was a very interesting idea, and he'd take it under advisement."

"In other words, go to hell."

"Yep. So I kept calling until he talked to me again and told me his accountant had told him my plan wasn't feasible. I asked for a meeting with him and his accountant and God and everybody, in which I would prove to him that he could turn this building and some others to his advantage by rehabbing them for low-income housing. He suddenly got a long-distance phone call on another line and told me his secretary would contact me."

"Still waiting?"

"Only in a sense. We've taken our campaign to the streets and to the media since then. But the press in this town—"

"Yeah, I know. We'll have a heat wave in the Arctic before those guys will openly criticize a local real estate big shot. You should be glad they gave you any publicity. And speaking of that, how come Kirkendahl hasn't sued you for slander yet?"

"Slander, hell, we've been working on libel for months, and nothing doing."

"You *want* to be sued?"

"Hell, yes! Think of the coverage!"

"Think of the expense!"

"Yeah, but once your back is against the wall, people rally round, you know? We'd raise a legal defense fund in no time, we'd probably pull a sympathetic jury, and we'd get the kind of publicity money can't buy."

I recognized the tone. It was the same one Franny had used in explaining why she'd taken a sledgehammer to an army Jeep at a Nevada missile site five years ago. Of course, she never got within slingshot distance of an actual missile and she served thirty days in jail. She got time off for singing peace songs day in and day out in her tone-deaf, ear-shattering wail, to an untuned guitar.

Something had been fluttering just out of my mind's eye and now it came into view.

"I don't suppose you know who does Kirkendahl's legal work?"

"Not me. We've never received so much as a warning, I'm sorry to say."

"So you don't know, for example, if Kirkendahl uses Graft, Graft, Feinstein and Waite?"

"No, I couldn't say. Why?"

Some people have tunnel vision and can see everything clearly within their limited field but wouldn't notice a rhinoceros standing one foot to the left.

"Look, McGann, maybe *you* didn't know that Betty was giving large anonymous gifts to Street People United, but her lawyer knew. So the question we should ask ourselves is who else knew?"

"Oh," he said, then, *"Oh!"*

"Kirkendahl had a vested interest in keeping you guys running on a shoestring. Suppose that Betty really did have a fortune somewhere out there." My gesture took in the chaos of SPU headquarters and the city beyond. "What would Kirkendahl do if he learned that Betty had begun to give away large amounts of money to SPU?"

"He'd *murder* her, the son of a bitch!" In his excitement, McGann whanged his knee on the corner of the file drawer.

He'd raised suspicion to an art form.

* * *

At home, Kevin grilled me while I mixed up a cake for Ben's birthday. Tomorrow Sharon's son, Ben, turned four and I was invited to his party. With a goddamned cake. Sharon labored under the delusion that all grannies like to bake cakes. It was related to the delusion that all grannies like to attend birthday parties with hordes of small children who will dribble melted ice cream on their best skirts, break their eardrums with screeching, and probably give them some virus that the elderly are defenseless against. I had a friend who got shingles that way. I'd sooner be trapped in a sweltering elevator with Margaret Thatcher and the Mouseketeers.

The fruits of the day's labors were spread out in front of him: two white-on-black photocopies of old newspaper articles, and one recent article that had been tucked inside one of the copies. The oldest was from 1978. It described a building fire in which the building was a total loss. The building was owned by Kirkendahl and Associates. The second was from 1981. It also described a fire in a downtown building owned by Kirkendahl and Associates. The newspaper clipping from last year told a different story. This one was about toxic wastes found in leaking drums in a storeroom in an old warehouse in Queensgate. The owner expressed shock at the discovery that he had suddenly become responsible for a clean-up operation that could cost more than twice what he'd paid for the run-down building six months before.

I suppose you'll want to know if I called the owner. I did. He bought the building from some outfit called Transstar. The Better Business Bureau had never heard of them. So I called the library. It took a while, but the business librarian finally came up with the information I needed: a list of company partners. Harold Waite and Edgar-goddamn-Kirkendahl were two of them. God bless the public library.

"So what do you make of these three articles? Betty was building a case against Kirkendahl?"

"Looks like it to me." I gave Sophie a light dusting of flour as I crossed the room to look over Kevin's shoulder.

"Yeah, but Mrs. C, if this is all she had, it looks like a pretty weak case to me. The guy may well be torching his own buildings, but two fires in three years don't seem all that suspicious when you consider the neighborhood and the conditions of some of the buildings he owns. And the toxic waste business may give him a bad reputation with the general public, but it's not actually illegal to sell a building housing that kind of stuff as long as you claim that you didn't know it was on the premises. Three articles don't constitute a motive for murder in my book."

I thought a moment. "But that's just it: how do we know there weren't more? Maybe she was carrying others around with her and left these in the office for safekeeping. Maybe she went to meet Kirkendahl promising to bring evidence with her. That could explain why she and Lucille were searched. Or maybe she was bluffing and hadn't found anything else, or hadn't gotten around to it. Maybe she never contacted Kirkendahl. Maybe he found out what she was up to somehow and went out of his way to bump into her on the bus."

"Yeah, but I thought you said Leon didn't recognize his picture."

"Yes, but Leon was looking at copies of old photographs. Maybe he just couldn't tell. After all, I wouldn't have recognized McGann from that picture. And the guy Leon saw had reasons to avoid being recognized."

"You mean the old fake mustache trick?"

"Well, I was thinking of something a little less dramatic. But yes, something like that."

"All right, so does this mean you've given up the treasure hunt?"

"Certainly not! A good piece of jewelry like that? I'd love to get my mitts on those rocks. I searched every inch of that goddamn office and didn't find anything. But the only way to strip that office down to the bare essentials would be to announce a garage sale. So no, I'm not one hundred percent sure there's nothing there."

"Well, I hope you didn't make it too complicated. There's always the possibility that this is a case like 'The Purloined Letter,' you know. Something hidden in plain sight. Like, say, anything resembling a necklace."

"You mean, the paperweight on the desk that turns out to be the Velazquez emerald? The rhinestones on the wall clock that turn out to be diamonds? The jar of Cremora filled with pearls?"

"Buried under the spider plant? A pearl taped to the underside of each typewriter key? A gold handprint ashtray or Statue of Liberty thermometer that turns out to be solid gold? The possibilities are endless."

"Yeah, and there's also the possibility that she sold the bloody necklace a long time ago."

"In which case she ought to have something more to show for it than a thousand bucks and a life lived out of shopping bags."

"Maybe she bet on the ponies. Hell, she might have done anything with it!" I slammed the cake pans into the oven and shoved the door closed. "Maybe I shouldn't be a detective, Kevin. Maybe I should be a nurse. Plenty of work, good pay—"

"Dirty bedpans, male chauvinist doctors, and cranky sick people. You'd hate it, Mrs. C. Too much like motherhood. No, listen, I think you're on the right track here. I do. Look at all you know now that you didn't know two weeks ago."

"But what am I supposed to do with it? I know too goddamn much, if you want to know the truth, and yet not enough."

He was making consoling noises when Alice stopped by to borrow the vacuum cleaner. She and Mel were pretty polite about it, actually, considering that most of what they vacuumed up was cat hair, which I strongly suspected of having sent their vacuum to the shop.

"Who's the new gray-and-white kitty?" she asked.

"That's Sophie practicing her undercover cat routine," I said.

"I thought maybe she had a cousin visiting. So how's the case going?"

Kevin and I took turns filling her in. When we showed her the newspaper clipping about the toxic waste, she raised her eyebrows.

"He sold this place in June of last year? What a snake!"

"Snakes, plural. He seems to have had company in this particular enterprise."

"You know about the state legislation, don't you?"

"What legislation?"

"About selling property housing toxic chemicals?" We shook our heads. "Well, it's designed to prevent just this kind of situation by making the lending institution responsible for clean-up. In other words, if you buy property and later discover toxic chemicals there, the bank that loaned you the money can be forced to pay for the clean-up."

"Really?"

"Sure. So the effect has been to induce lending institutions to inspect property very carefully before they agree to a loan."

"But when did this law go into effect?"

"Just this year. But they first started talking about it last year, and your pal Kirkendahl is just the kind of guy to have a buddy in the legislature who'd be sure he knew it was in the works so that he could dump any property like this before it was too late. As far as that goes, pending legislation isn't secret, and I'm sure the Kirkendahl real estate conglomerate keeps its collective eye on those things."

"That wouldn't be illegal, though, would it?" Kevin asked. "If he sold the property before the law went into effect, I mean." He scooped up Sophie, dangled her over the table, and blew. A small white cloud descended on the table. And the floor, chairs, countertop, Al, and me.

"No, it may have been unethical, but it wasn't illegal, if that's what happened. After all, people like Kirkendahl probably pay for that kind of information all the time in contributions to political campaigns."

"So it's still not a motive for murder." I heaved a sigh, and Sophie was again sprinkled with white fallout.

"But Mrs. C, why are you so glum? Where motives are concerned, you've got a whole shopping bag full. You don't need another motive. What you need is means and opportunity."

"What I need," I said, coughing from the flour that coated my throat, "is a note from my mother excusing me from my grandson's birthday party."

CHAPTER 14

Personally, I thought Kevin was too damned optimistic. *I* hadn't even met the person with the best motive yet — the heiress. That is, she had the best motive if there was anything to inherit, or if she thought there was. But before I could meet her, I had a date with Stephen Grunewald. Kevin had pleaded for permission to come along. I think he was hoping I'd want him to disguise himself as a cabbie, but I don't think it would have been very convincing.

Anyway, it was just as well he was coming, as it turned out. At the birthday party I had received a vicious kick in the shin from a little girl. She hadn't meant to hurt me; she was aiming at Ben. Afterward, Ben told me in confidence that she was his girlfriend.

"Does she know it?" I said.

So there I was, limping along, with a bruise the size of a dinner plate on my shin. I could have worn pants, but the day was hot. And since I was limping anyway, I assumed it would be better to demonstrate that the limp was justified. I hoped he thought I'd gotten it in a tussle with a dangerous crook.

"You're Professor Grunewald?" I said when he answered my knock. "But you don't look anything like your picture!" Tact is my middle name.

"Oh — the one on the book jacket? No, I don't, do I? Of course, that was ages ago. 'I grow old,' as Prufrock says. But it didn't look much like me at the time either. Everyone said so."

Grunewald was the third suspect to fall within the height range specified by Leon Jakes, as interpreted by me. And he had a full beard and mustache, lighter than it looked in the photograph. Surely Leon would have mentioned a beard if the man he'd spotted had worn one, but on the other hand, the guy could have grown two beards or shaved them off since then. Grunewald was wearing spiffy khaki pants, very wrinkled, a short-sleeve white shirt and sandals. He smelled of tobacco.

His was a spacious corner office in an old building that smelled faintly of moldy paper. Against one wall stood a television set on a stand with a VCR. Next to it sat something that looked like another kind of audiovisual aid, as they were called when my kids were in school. Over Grunewald's desk was a poster showing Humphrey Bogart sitting alone at a table, drinking, agonized because "of all the gin joints in all the towns," et cetera. There were other posters around the room, mostly half-hidden behind books and file cabinets and crap, some in print I couldn't read or featuring names I couldn't pronounce. Kevin was in seventh heaven, I could tell.

I introduced Kevin, who offered his condolences on Betty's death. Grunewald strode across the room and cleared the top of a tall file cabinet with one sweep of his arm, exposing a poster for *Satan's Handmaiden.*

"I found out about it when the reporter called me from Channel Nine. I'd read about the murdered vagrant in the paper, of course, and I had perhaps better reason than most to connect her with Betty, knowing as I did that Betty had hit the skids, as it were. But I just didn't think. I can't believe she's dead." He sighed and gazed reverently at Betty's image. So we looked, too. In the poster, Betty was busy vamping Rudolph Valentino, no slouch himself where women were concerned. Her eyes appeared to be outlined in black magic marker, and you could have hung out a load of wash on her eyelashes.

She had a hand tucked under her chin like Cleopatra and her fingers were loaded down with rings. I scrutinized the jewelry, you can bet, but I couldn't tell if it was real or fake. She was wearing something slinky, and Rudolph seemed to be slinking along behind her. His eyes were probably smoldering, but you couldn't tell in the poster.

"She was incredibly beautiful," said Kevin.

"Yes," said Grunewald. "In her youth she was said to have been one of the wonders of the world. What a tragic life, a tragic ending — old age, illness, loss of beauty, destitution, then violent death."

"I think she was a goddamn wonder up to the day she died." Grunewald was pissing me off with his patronizing attitude. Everybody's a fucking scriptwriter. "She'd survived on the streets for years with her dignity intact, she had friends, and she'd become politically active."

"Ah, yes, but once . . ." He shrugged as if comparison were useless.

"Once, according to your own biography, she achieved Hollywood stardom and with it all the pressures and anxieties that come with the territory. Insomnia, diet pills, tranquilizers, alcohol, general purpose amphetamines, and childlessness — all to keep her career afloat so that she could continue to present the public with that goddamn illusion of perfection. Am I right?"

"Oh, that was no illusion. She was just as beautiful off camera as on."

I turned away from Grunewald and made a face at Kevin.

"We've both read your book, Professor, and enjoyed it immensely. But as Ms. Caliban told you over the telephone—" He usually calls me "Ms." in public, a well-trained boy.

"She is trying to help the police investigate Betty Grumbacher's murder. We were hoping you might provide us with additional information or insight."

"I'd be happy to help if I can." He waved us toward two chairs. "I think I can say in all honesty that I am the world's expert on the life and career of Leda Marrs." He sat down and began to fiddle with his pipe.

"One of the matters we're trying to resolve concerns Betty's financial state at the time of her death," Kevin continued. "There is a will leaving everything to her daughter."

"Her daughter, eh?" He began to puff and looked at us over his pipe. "I always suspected she had a child. I believe I discuss the issue in Chapter Five, don't I?" Puff. "Tricky business, that — the publishers were concerned about possible lawsuits, so it's all couched in the most careful of language. 'It may be true that,' 'One can't help but speculate whether,' 'One is tempted to suggest' — that sort of thing. So she had a daughter. Living in the city?"

"In Montgomery. But the real question is whether or not she had anything to leave her daughter. I'd be interested in your opinion on that."

He tipped his chair back and gazed upward at the ceiling.

"A provocative question, that. She may have, and then again, she may not have. She had ample opportunity in her life to accumulate a fortune, but also ample opportunity to spend it."

"Both in the twenties, I assume you mean?"

"Oh, yes. Oh, God, yes. There was nothing coming in later, assuming, of course, an absence of investments. But investments were certainly possible, if not plausible."

"What do you mean?" I asked. Kevin wore a fixed smile that suggested he was determined to be polite. Or it may have meant that he wasn't going to risk opening his mouth for fear of telling this jerk what an asshole he was. But that's more my style than his.

"Ah, well. If you've read my book, you must have some idea. Why, in her heyday I expect she received hundreds of dollars' worth of presents in any given week — fur coats, automobiles, jewelry, crystal, expensive wines, perfumes, purebred puppies, even a race horse named Wages of Sin. If the press printed a story about a puppy one week, she'd receive five jeweled collars in the mail the next. If she was shown drinking champagne in a press photo, she'd receive fifty cases of the stuff before the month was out. This in the midst of Prohibition, you must remember. She always said she was drinking soda water out of a champagne glass."

"Didn't she give some of it away?"

"Ah, but my dear Mrs. Caliban, you might as well ask if the Shah of Iran didn't give something to charity. I suspect it's hard for us to imagine the magnitude of such a fortune in gifts."

"But she would have paid taxes on it too, right?" This from Kevin, who was too young to remember a time when income taxes were one of life's minor considerations.

"Certainly. But one must remember that the income tax was considerably less then than it is now, and in 1926 it was actually lowered. No, I rather doubt that taxes put any significant dent in her fortune. I believe it was her lifestyle that finally ran her aground, if you will."

"You mean she spent every penny she got?"

"I expect so, yes. And you must remember that her popularity faded in the late twenties. Money to pay a mortgage on an eighteen-room mansion didn't come so easily in those days. Especially if one was drinking half one's salary and spending a good part on clothes. One press report claimed that the star owned twenty-three negligees. I can't verify the report, but I wouldn't be surprised."

"So if she drank when drinking was illegal, did she ever get in trouble with the law?"

"Good Lord, no. In Los Angeles County? It would have been unthinkable. I should say, of course, that there were a few automobile mishaps that seem to have been alcohol-related. In such cases I believe it was customary for the studio to intervene with the police, though certainly that was much more common later when the studios gained more power."

"Did *she* tell you about these 'mishaps,' as you call them?"

"Oh, no. She never spoke to me. That is, she never consented to be interviewed for the book. I believe the Introduction—"

Neither of us helped him out, the old slyboots. The Introduction intimated that Miss Marrs was something of a recluse, unwilling to discuss the past. But it never came right out and said that she had refused to have anything to do with the book. I began to wonder about Lucille.

"But you did interview Miss Shelton?"

"Lucille Shelton, you mean? Yes, I spoke to her. 'Interview' is perhaps not the appropriate word, but she did give me some useful information."

So Lucille had sent him packing, too. Good for her.

"And you don't believe that Betty Grumbacher died with a fortune stashed away somewhere to leave to her daughter?"

"Now, I can only venture to express an opinion, and in my opinion, it is highly unlikely. I suppose the will is a recent one?"

"Dated last year," I affirmed.

He nodded. "I see the problem. However, I think it plausible that Betty may have wished to convey the impression of wealth to the daughter she once abandoned. That would certainly account for the will. She would imagine that the daughter would simply assume that the fortune is hidden away somewhere and will never be found. Then, too, Betty's mental health was not always sound, as I expect you know. Who knows what her reasons might have been for drawing up such a document?"

He was pissing me off again, yammering about mental health as if Betty were bonkers.

"And the Velazquez emerald?" This time it was Kevin who pounced.

"Ah, yes, the Velazquez. What about it?"

"Didn't you make any effort to determine whether it had been sold on the black market?"

"Well, naturally, I made inquiries. Unfortunately, university professors don't make the kind of money necessary to prosecute such inquiries successfully. Nor do we move in the appropriate circles. But that goes without saying. No, I should require a great deal of time and money to answer that question. Perhaps I should ask the National Endowment for the Humanities if it would be willing to fund such an enterprise." He chuckled, wit incarnate.

"Betty seems to have been the marrying kind, according to your book."

"She was and she wasn't. Certainly she entertained many admirers whom she never married, including perhaps her daughter's father."

"Yes, but you describe three marriages in your book."

"Quite true. The disastrous first marriage to William Buckner, who seems to have been employed as a mechanic of some kind at the local printing plant. Then she fell in love with a bit player from *The Beautiful Martyr*, Raymond Wilcox, Jr., whose career stumbled and died shortly thereafter. Then there was a dashing young apprentice cameraman, David Driscoll Lloyd, who was a year younger than she."

"And you don't think any of them was her daughter's father?"

"Pure speculation on my part, but I don't think so." He started pointing his pipe at me. "She disappeared for about eleven good months in 1926, and I noted in the book that either she had brought a pregnancy to term or she was recuperating from a botched abortion. I didn't envision her as the motherly type, you see, although one can never tell, can one? In any event, she was divorced from Wilcox at the time and not yet married to Lloyd. Practically speaking, either man could have been the father. But so could Carter Eggleston, the railroad magnate. And so could Sheik Ali Khabril, he of the Velazquez emerald. And so could any number of other men."

"All right. But if she married so often, why not marry the father of the child if she was pregnant? She doesn't seem to have had reservations about matrimony, whatever her track record." This was Kevin again, caught in a time warp.

"Well, Eggleston was already married, if you recall from the book. And divorce — well, it was hardly common, for all the screen time Von Stroheim devoted to it. I mean, divorce was for movie stars, but Eggleston wasn't a movie star, he was a businessman. The sheik was engaged to a suitable Arabian princess, according to time-honored tradition, and he married his fiancée with pomp and ceremony in 1928. I believe he gave her a perfect strand of pearls as a wedding present, but rumor had it that the necklace couldn't hold a candle to the Velazquez emerald, so to speak."

"You say in the book that you couldn't find out whether she had ever married again."

"No, I couldn't. Odd that people can keep so many secrets when they wish."

"But you must have checked county records?"

"Certainly. I checked under Grumbacher, Buckner, Wilcox, and Lloyd, both in Hamilton and Los Angeles counties, and came up dry. But she married Buckner in a third county, remember. And she may have done it again."

"You thought she did."

"Well, as this young man pointed out, she *did* have a record. Marriage can be habit-forming, or so I'm told. I should have expected her to marry again. And again. And again, as it were."

"How many of the ex-husbands are still alive?"

"Oh, only one, as far as I know, and that's Wilcox, who's in a nursing home in Duluth. I'm afraid it wouldn't do you a bit of good to talk to the old boy. He wasn't terribly sharp when I interviewed him over ten years ago. If he hasn't kicked the bucket yet, he must be utterly gaga."

It always sounded suspicious when somebody warned you away from a possible witness. I made a mental note to track down Wilcox.

"Do you have any theories about Betty's murder?"

He studied the ceiling again.

"I'm afraid, Mrs. Caliban, that I'm much more competent to interpret the past than the present. I really couldn't say. Naturally I've speculated. But no, I haven't really reached any conclusions."

"I gather she wasn't actually homeless when you wrote the book?"

"She had a tiny apartment in some dilapidated building downtown, since demolished. Dim, smelly hallways, cockroaches, peeling paint — that kind of thing." His face registered distaste, as if he'd just caught a whiff of a teenager's socks after soccer practice. "But no, as far as I know, she wasn't homeless, unless the apartment really belonged to someone else." He paused. "The Channel 9 reporter indicated that she'd become active in some organization recently, a kind of rabble-rousing group for the homeless."

"Street People United."

He nodded. "One meets such odd people in those kinds of organizations. They attract a certain kind of personality. I've wondered whether she didn't get in with the wrong kind of crowd there. Once a certain kind of person gets stirred up, there is no telling what might happen."

Kevin cut me off before I could respond.

"I see you have some videotapes of the Marrs films over there on the shelf. Ms. Caliban has never seen one. Do you suppose we could borrow a couple? We'd be very careful with them, and promise to bring them right back."

He frowned. "Well, I don't normally loan them out. I've only one copy of each. But if you think it might help, I don't see that I can refuse. I only ask that you take special care of them in this heat. You must not, please, under *any* circumstances, leave them on a car seat or a sunny windowsill. I'd also appreciate it if you'd promise just to run them through once on forward, and then rewind. No back and forth, reverse and fast forward, you understand."

We promised.

"You'd think that prick was handing over the Velazquez jewels himself," I expostulated once we reached the sidewalk.

CHAPTER 15

The next day I spent doing laundry. Even detectives have to have clean clothes now and then. They never discuss this subject in mystery novels. Where does Spenser get his clean underwear? Inquiring minds want to know.

So I shook the kitties out of the dirty towels and moved the whole damn mountain downstairs to the basement. The washer gave the equivalent of a metallic gasp of astonishment when I turned it on. What the hell. If the basement flooded, I could always open a wading pool for neighborhood kids.

Mel stopped in while I was chasing dust bunnies around the bedroom with the vacuum cleaner. She wanted to know if she could build a workbench in the basement. Some people know how to pick tenants and some people don't.

"So," she said, as we sat in the kitchen drinking iced tea, "does this guy Grunewald get a place on your list of suspects?"

"For my money, he does. Kevin says I shouldn't be swayed by his un-magnetic personality, but I don't think that's it. The point is he knows more about Betty Grumbacher than anybody living, by his own admission. And he knew Lucille, presumably knew where to find her."

"Got a motive?"

"A what?" I was momentarily tuned in to the vibrations underfoot. You would have thought I was setting off a hydrogen bomb in the basement. I'd seen Sadie headed for the front door, looking back over her shoulder as if she thought the Big Earthquake had finally hit southern Ohio.

"A motive? You know, the things that people lie, cheat, steal and kill for."

"Oh, that. Yes, well, the way I see it, Grunewald knows something he's not telling. For one thing, he's too damn certain that Betty had spent her fortune. It could be thinly veiled contempt of the kind he specializes in, but it could be a ruse to throw me off the scent. Say he knows she had a fortune, found out when he wrote the book, and figured out where she kept it."

"But why kill her, then? And why now? Why not years ago?"

"Okay, maybe he didn't know where it was. Maybe he spent the past ten years looking for it, then decided, or happened on an opportunity, to make her give him the information. When she wouldn't tell him, he killed her and went after Lucille. You wouldn't know from the book that he knew that Lucille was Betty's best friend, but I bet he did know."

"So in this scenario, the nine hundred-dollar contribution to SPU has no significance."

"It may have. Suppose Harold Waite tipped off Grunewald. Or suppose Betty mentioned the contribution herself. Maybe Grunewald wasn't sure about the fortune before, until he heard about the donation."

"So you have to find out whether Waite knew Grunewald?"

"I suppose. But that may be hard to discover, and ultimately not all that significant."

"Let me guess: you're going to sneak into Grunewald's house and go through his clothes hamper looking for bloodstains."

"Are you kidding? Bloodstains are a snap to clean. Hardly in the same league with spaghetti sauce and cat piss."

"Men don't know that."

"True. They don't have occasion to be reminded once a month."

"Then what's your next move?"

"Well, I haven't yet completed my list of suspects. I'm going to call Helen Prescott today. She can't have been the man Leon saw, but there may be a Mr. Helen Prescott — father or son."

"Anyway, I thought you were hot on the trail of this Kirkendahl guy and his real estate misadventures. At least you *know* that he knew Waite and could have heard about the donation."

"Yeah, but I don't have much to build a case on, as your astute roomie pointed out. Unless he had his own buildings torched, which will be hard to prove at this late date, he hasn't done anything illegal. At least, it's not illegal to sell property that turns out to be a toxic waste dump unless someone can prove that he knew about the chemicals. Now if he torched a building and someone died in the fire, we'd really have him."

"But maybe he did. Maybe the three clippings you have don't tell the whole story."

"That's the trouble. I don't know. She may have had more, or she may not. And speaking of clippings, I'd like to know where the hell that flatfoot Eddie Landau is with my photocopies of the contents of Betty's safe deposit box. You'd think a cop could pull off one tiny goddamn theft without spending a week casing the joint and planning the heist."

The washing machine hit the spin cycle running. Sidney appeared in the doorway and voiced his opinion that someone ought to do something to make the house quit shaking before we all ended up in Kansas. I promised to look into the matter and descended to the basement. The washer was foaming at the mouth. I stood and regarded it from a distance, which I considered the most prudent course of action. At last it lurched to a stop and gave a shudder of relief. It had traveled four feet from its original location. I decided to give the dryer a break and cut the load in half. Everything was covered with tiny scraps of tissue from a pocket I had forgotten to turn. A red washcloth had dyed all of my underwear pink.

Of such events are bad days made. Spenser didn't know what he was missing.

I had yard work to do, so I slapped on a little suntan lotion and went out to do battle with the gnats, flies, fleas, and mosquitoes.

You may wonder why I'm telling you all this. You may think it irrelevant to the matter at hand. What you don't realize is that we detectives are always thinking — always, even when we're in the john. When somebody pays for our time (which so far nobody had offered to do in my case), they really get double time, since we don't charge for what Franny would call "processing" time.

So I went out to the yard, communed with the wildlife and weeds, and processed. What did I have so far? For suspects, I had Harold Waite, Edgar Kirkendahl, Stephen Grunewald, the unknown Prescotts, Bill McGann, and, for good measure, Betty's pals down at St. Francis. In all cases, there was a possible financial motive. Hell, even the street people could have a financial motive. How did I know that Betty wasn't killed for the contents of her shopping bags — the knit caps, aluminum cans, stray socks and such? One man's coal was another man's diamond. That would mean that Lucille was killed either for the same reason, or because she knew who Betty's killer was. Maybe she'd seen somebody wearing a sock she recognized. Unless Lucille's murder was completely unrelated, in which case I would have to solve it separately.

I reached under a bush and struck fur. It was Sidney, out collecting fleas.

"Waite seems to me to be the key figure in the plot," I told Sidney, presenting a weed for him to sniff so that he could see I wasn't pulling up catnip. "He's the only one so far who knew that Betty had started to give her money away. Unless Bill McGann knew, of course. And I admit it seems funny that McGann didn't even suspect the source, knowing Betty as well as he did. Could she have resisted the temptation to hint around? And let him know that there might be more coming? But if she did that, why would he kill her? And it's not likely that he'd tell Kirkendahl about the donation. But a guy like Kirkendahl has ways of finding out. Which brings us back to Harold Waite. If he's in this alone, what does it mean? That he's secretly milked the estate of its assets and managed to cover his tracks so well that nobody even knows that a fortune once existed? Is that possible? For a smart lawyer, my guess is that it would be, but is Waite a smart lawyer? Smarter than Betty? And what about Grunewald? Did he find out that the Velazquez emerald was slipping away just as he was about to get his hands on it? Ditto the Prescotts, who are probably just a nice, unassuming, unsuspecting couple. We'll see."

From inside the house, the dryer made a noise like an air raid siren.

CHAPTER 16

Scratch that about the Prescotts being an unassuming couple. I thought Mrs. Prescott sounded nice, if a bit bewildered, over the phone. But they lived in a house that could easily be converted into a hangar for the Starship *Enterprise.* Montgomery is not known for its modest cottages. It took me a quarter of a goddamn hour just to drive up the driveway.

I took one look at Helen Prescott and I knew who her father was. It was quite a shock. You would have thought the possibility would have occurred to me before — that she would resemble her father, that is, but it hadn't. Now I confronted a woman taller than I was with coarse black hair pulled back, dark eyes, dark skin, and a prominent nose. A handsome woman. The daughter of an Arab sheik.

She ushered me into a living room that was some decorator's idea of what a living room should be. She seated me on a sofa my cats would have made mincemeat out of. I began to worry that I might be trailing cat hair. I was glad I'd decided on hose and pumps.

"This has all been such a surprise to us, Mrs. Caliban, as I'm sure you can imagine. I have the sense that I gained and lost a mother at one fell swoop, if you know what I mean."

She had a pleasant voice, one that went with the living room. She must have been about my age, but she had a youthful look attributable either to her ethnic heritage or to her wealth, I guessed. "Still, I can't really think of her as my mother, since my adopted mother has always been mother to me. She'd told me I was adopted, of course, but said she didn't know who my real mother was, and it didn't matter to me, really. I mean, I never missed having a mother, so the most I could feel was a kind of vague curiosity. When I learned that my real mother had been murdered, and what the circumstances were, of course I felt badly for her, but I can't say that I grieved."

"Is your adopted mother still alive?"

"No, she passed away four years ago."

"I assume the police told you about Leda Marrs."

"Oh, yes. I went right down to the bookstore to buy the biography, but it was out of print, so I had to go to the library. Have you read it? It's fascinating, don't you think? Naturally, I felt curious about who my father was. I confess that now all this has come up, that's a mystery I'd like to solve."

I studied her. Was it really possible that she couldn't see her Arab heritage in her face? Or was it just that she was used to her face, and unused to seeing it objectively?

"I suppose the police told you about the will."

She smiled. "Yes, they did, and I'm grateful to her for her generosity, even if she had nothing to leave, poor thing. I wish I'd known about her situation. Perhaps Harrison and I — Harrison is my husband — he's out playing golf. Perhaps Harrison and I could have done something for her."

"So you had no idea that you were the legatee under the terms of your real mother's will — your birth mother, that is?"

"No. How could I? I didn't have a clue who she was."

"And did the police indicate that they had any reason to believe your mother might have been a very wealthy woman?"

"No, why?" Mild surprise, I'd say.

"As Leda Marrs, your mother received, in addition to what in those days was considered a spectacular salary, several truckloads' worth of expensive gifts from her admirers. Among other things, she was supposedly given a priceless emerald necklace by an Arab sheik."

"Oh, I remember him from the book. He married a princess."

"Right." Could anybody be this dense? I tried to put myself in her shoes and failed. For one thing, her shoes were worth half my mortgage payment. "So the big question seems to be, what happened to all this material wealth she accumulated in her youth?"

"I see what you mean. But I just assumed she spent it all. Didn't the book say that she was in hospitals a lot, and that her mother died of a long illness? As the wife of a doctor, I'm in a position to know what illnesses cost. And every time malpractice insurance goes up, patient bills go up. It stands to reason."

I refrained from saying that it only stood to reason if you were standing in a two-hundred-thousand-dollar house that you happened to own. Profit margins were important to these folks.

"So you never had an inkling that you could be an heiress?"

"Good heavens, no!"

"And your husband?"

"My husband what?" She looked perplexed.

"He never suspected that you might be an heiress?"

"Oh, I don't think so. He's not very concerned about money anyway. He loves his work."

This was so patently false when I surveyed the room that I had to bite my tongue to keep from laughing. Somebody in this house had to care about money or I was Ingrid Bergman.

"Do you have children?"

"Yes, our eldest practices at Cedars-Sinai, and our youngest is a resident at Johns Hopkins. Our middle child is the renegade — she's a chemist at Dow."

"I'm a better doctor than I am a golfer, so I'd better love my work," a voice boomed from the doorway.

Prescott was a medium tall man — yes, shorter than Leon — with a paunch. He was dressed for golf in a pair of plaid

Bermuda shorts and a knit shirt with a fucking alligator over his heart. His face was flushed. Whether from the sun, the nineteenth hole, or both, I couldn't tell. He blinked a lot and from time to time opened his eyes wide, sort of like Jimmy Carter, so I figured he wore contact lenses. He had large paw-like hands — I noticed when he shook mine. He kept hold of it and patted it, winking at me and asking me whether I'd dug up the fortune that his wife had inherited from her deceased mother. A sample of his bedside manner.

I said that I'd come to ask her where to look. He laughed at that. He had the kind of laugh that makes people turn around in restaurants. He went behind the bar and started rattling bottles. There was some good-natured banter between husband and wife over whether I would be forced to try some special concoction of his. She won, and he fixed me a gin and tonic instead. It was about half and half, with a whisper of lime.

"Seriously, now, Mrs. Caliban," he said as he settled back on the sofa with an arm around his wife. "This business of Helen's really takes the cake. Don't you think so? Imagine learning that your real mother was a vagrant who has been murdered and left you everything, which turns out to be nothing. And then finding out that she had once been a movie star. Why, if they put this plot into one of those paperback novels, nobody would believe it, would they?"

"So you don't believe that Betty had a fortune to leave?"

"Well, it stands to reason she didn't, doesn't it? If she did, why would she be out on the streets?"

"Maybe because she wanted to leave her daughter a fortune."

Dr. Prescott shook his head. "That's a bit far-fetched, isn't it? I expect I've treated enough women over the years to be something of an expert in female psychology, and I'll allow you that women will do the damndest things, all right, especially where children are concerned. But I won't buy that one."

"What's your medical specialty, doctor?"

"Gynecology. I used to do obstetrics, too, but the goddamn malpractice insurance went through the roof, so I threw in the towel. Don't get me started on insurance!"

"I won't. I understand you put two kids through medical school and one through graduate school, too. That must have been expensive." Cat Caliban. Master of subtlety.

He could have been offended if he saw where I was leading him, but he just laughed again. "Don't I know it! The kids all contributed, of course, but the cost of becoming a doctor has tripled since I went through. I said to Helen we might as well move into a tent and be done with it!

"No, seriously," he continued, after a moment, as he tried to compose his face into a serious expression, "I feel for the old girl — Helen's mother. After all, I've got a lot to be grateful to her for." He patted his wife's knee. "I wish we could help catch the bastard who did her in. I'd love to get my hands on him. But — there you have it. We didn't even know if Helen's mother was alive, much less who or where she was. Doesn't look like we're much use at all."

"Do you know Harold Waite?" Attack Cat. Was there a flicker?

He turned to his wife. They both frowned and looked thoughtful. "Harold Waite? Do we know him? Hang on. Is he the attorney that's handling this Grumbacher estate — that is, the nonexistent Grumbacher estate?"

"That's right."

"I've heard of him. Must've handled some legal business for somebody I know. Can't say I've run into him, though, that I can remember. Helen accuses me of having a mind like a sieve. I tell her it's just focused on important things." He laughed again. "But this Waite fellow — with a downtown firm, is he?" I nodded. "Don't see much of those fellows out here in the sticks, and we don't get downtown these days as much as we used to." He laughed again. Maybe he thought it was funny to refer to his upper-middle-class neighborhood as "the sticks."

"You don't have an affiliation with any of the city hospitals?"

"Oh, well, yes, if it comes to that. I do some work at Christ. But they're not exactly downtown, either. I meant that I didn't go into town the way I used to for lunch or anything. Truth is, Mrs. Caliban, I'm getting old. Don't go anywhere the way I used to." He laughed again. His wife smiled and shook her head at him. "No, I've deliberately slowed down my practice. Gives me more time to spend on the links." He took an imaginary swing of a golf club.

"Harold Waite's an older gentleman, too," I said evenly, not to be deterred. "Maybe you met him when you used to go downtown in your youth."

"Could be. Could very well be. Obviously didn't make a big impression on me."

"How about Edgar Kirkendahl? Have you ever met him?"

"The real estate investor? Yes, now I have run into him on occasion. I know him to speak to. The rubber chicken circuit, you understand." He laughed and went to take another slug of his drink, and found it empty. He stood up and reached for my glass, but I shook my head. As he headed for the bar, his wife gave me a wry smile and a shrug.

"Now how is he involved in this Grumbacher business, I wonder? Don't tell me the old fox had secretly invested a million in downtown real estate while masquerading as a bag lady?"

"No, but she was involved in street demonstrations against Kirkendahl. She was part of an organization that wanted him to rehab some of his empty buildings to house the homeless."

"You don't say? Now I had the impression the old bird was cuckoo. I'm surprised to hear she was involved in something like that. You know, I think they've got something there, too. Of course, it goes without saying that an investor like Kirkendahl has to get a fair return on his property. But there might be a way to do it and come out ahead, what with all these federal grants they're throwing around these days. He ought to check into that. Might make more housing those poor bastards than taking a tax loss. Of course, you don't know what kind of tenants they'd be. Upkeep might run high."

"I still think he ought to consider it," Helen put in. "Between all the vacant office space downtown, and the empty apartment buildings, you'd think we could find a way to avoid having people like my mother sleeping in the gutters."

"Honey, by all accounts, your mother had a screw loose. She probably *liked* sleeping in the gutters." He winked at me.

"But Mrs. Caliban said she went to one of those demonstrations. That doesn't sound to me like she liked being homeless."

"Well," he appeased her, "it's probably foolish of us to sit here and speculate. We don't know what these folks are like."

They're just like you, you arrogant jerk; they want a nice place to live and good food to eat and a good education for their kids. They aren't brothers from another planet, I thought.

"Some of these people — why, they do feel entitled to a government handout. And the women — they know that as long as they keep having babies, they can count on Uncle Sam to take care of them."

You'd think a former O.B. would be smarter on this score. But in my experience, most of them don't know shit about women. Pregnancy provides only the most blatant example of what is wrong with the medical profession, especially as practiced by men: whatever it is you've got, they've never had it, so they don't think it's serious. Poverty is something else they've never had, so needless to say, they never tried to raise kids on ADC. He blathered on while I imagined what Betty would have said if she could have met her son-in-law. Maybe she had met him. Maybe that's why she'd pulled a knife.

When I got an opportunity to get a word in edgewise, I found that I didn't have anything more to say. Or rather, I had a lot to say, but I was on my good behavior, virtue thick on my tongue like Pepto-Bismol. As they walked me to the door, I had an inspiration.

"I wonder, Mrs. Prescott. Your mother was so fond of you — the will proves that. And it also proves that she knew where you were. I can't believe that your adoptive mother didn't know who your real mother — your birth mother, that is — who she was."

"Well, I suppose it's possible, but my mother and I were very close. I don't know why she would have lied to me."

"Oh, I can imagine reasons. It may have been Betty's stipulation after all. Maybe your mother promised Betty never to let you know who she was. But what I'm wondering is this: could she really have avoided seeing you or contacting you all those years when she was clearly thinking about you? I assume you've seen her picture — not just a police photograph, but the pictures in the Grunewald book."

"Yes, and you want to know if I recognize her. Let me get the book and I'll look again. You know, it never occurred to me that I might have met her sometime, but you may be right." She dashed off, and her husband dragged me off to show me the view from the deck. She returned, frowning at the book in her hand, shaking her head. "I'm sorry, Mrs. Caliban, she just doesn't look at all familiar to me. If I met her, it must have been in passing."

"Do you remember ever receiving any particularly odd phone calls? Or anything odd in the mail? Any gifts from an unknown party?"

"No, I can't think of anything unusual, except — well, now *that* was odd. I'd forgotten about the champagne."

"What champagne?" Her husband looked at her as if she'd been holding out on him.

"Well, you remember the bottle of champagne we were given for our wedding, and we couldn't figure out who it came from? And you said it was from my secret admirer, *and* you said that whoever he was, he must have been fond of me because it was such good champagne. Well, it just occurred to me that I also received a bottle of champagne for my twenty-first birthday. We could never figure out who it was from. We found it on the front porch, as if it had been delivered while we were gone, in a brown box as if it had been sent through the mail, only it couldn't have been, of course. I don't know whether it was good champagne or not; I'm afraid I didn't know anything about it at the time. And I thought my boyfriend sent it, or one of my brothers, but nobody would admit to it. Do you think—" She looked at me intently. "Do you think my mother sent it?"

"I think it quite possible."

Shades of *Stella Dallas*: a mother gives up her daughter so that the girl can have a better life, and stands in the rain watching her daughter's wedding through a window. What my mother used to call a three-hankie flick.

CHAPTER 17

I stepped on a brown envelope as I came through the door. It had my name on it, nothing else. I scrutinized it before I slipped my hand inside. I'd read about those booby traps that blew you into confetti as soon as you opened something up, and my momma didn't raise no boobies. What I got instead was dusty black-and-white photocopies of some old newspaper clippings, blurry. Goddamn, you want anything done right you got to do it yourself. Proper use of copy machines wasn't covered in police training.

I sat down at the kitchen table with my magnifying glass — a present from Franny when she found out I was turning detective. All the clippings were reviews of Leda Marrs films. The first reviewed *The Beautiful Martyr*, Betty's first big role. It featured an obligatory paragraph on the wholesome good looks of Blanche Sweet, then noted: "But Miss Sweet's charming performance is almost overshadowed by the sultry seductiveness of the newest female vampire to appear on the screen, Leda Marrs, who plays the treacherous Sapphira with serpentine abandon. Once Sapphira coils herself round the heart of the hero, the Christian cause is lost. We are reminded of the antics of that most successful of vamps, Miss Theda

Bara." That was all, as far as Betty was concerned, and I wondered if there was something here I was missing. I examined the article for any marks that Betty might have made, but the goddamn glass on the Xerox machine had been so filthy it was hard to tell.

There was a large circle in evidence — about the size of a coffee mug. What kind of slobs set coffee mugs down on a Xerox machine? No wonder the conviction rate was down. Inside the circle was a cast list. Important or not? I didn't recognize any of the names except Betty's and Blanche Sweet's, but Betty could have been married to one of them for all I knew. Probably not Blanche Sweet. I spotted two marks which might have been underlinings, or they might have been hairs stuck to the glass, both of them faint and crooked. One appeared under the word "Roman." *Shit,* I thought, *don't tell me she has an account in a Roman bank*. Or maybe she got married once in Rome, or had a Roman husband, or a husband named "Roman" as in Polanski. Or maybe it's short for romance. The other word was "set." Here, the reviewer was waxing enthusiastic about the realistic set, the Coliseum and catacombs and all. Roman set. What the hell did that mean? Maybe "set" was somebody's initials. Or maybe she had the Velazquez emerald reset in Rome. I was particularly fond of this last theory and decided to mull it over some more later.

The second article reviewed *Cleopatra of Egypt*, and I recognized Betty in the accompanying picture, bad copy though it was. I double-checked the first article, but it was Blanche Sweet who was in the picture. I squinted at Betty decked out like Cleopatra and suddenly my heart did a broad jump. Was that a line of duplicated fuzz around her neck or was she wearing an emerald necklace? I decided she was wearing something, but of course it was hard to tell in black and white. Emeralds, schmemeralds, she was sporting something the size of a baby's fist, artfully dangled above her fashionably discreet cleavage, and whatever it was, it made the snake wrapped around her forehead look like a coil of Play-Doh. There were so many little black spots on this copy it looked like the Arizona desert after a meteor shower. Was "jewels" underlined or was it my imagination? Ditto "city." Ditto "queen." Was this a veiled reference to the jewels hidden somewhere in Cincinnati, the Queen City of the West? If so, where the hell were they? Stuck to the underside of a seat on a Queen City Metro bus? Half the business establishments in the city were named after the Queen City. Had she sold the jewels to Queen City Jewelers? Pawned them at the Queen City Pawnshop? Was there any way I could get my hands on the originals of these damn photocopies before I made a complete ass of myself?

The last article was about *Wages of Sin*. Betty was cutting her eyes at Wallace Beery in a two-shot, and he was looking somewhat manic. I made a mental note to check and see if Wally was still alive, and if he ever looked that way in real life. Here, the cast list included Lucille Thornbush playing a character called "Delilah," surely a maid. I thought of Louise Beavers in *Imitation of Life*, forced to gain weight and speak with a Southern accent, and saddled with that name — Delilah. No wonder Lucille gave up on Hollywood. Her name would always appear in the small print. She would never be accepted, respected, challenged with an interesting role, allowed to expand her range as an actress. Her best bet would have been to hold out until they began to make those all-Black musicals in the late twenties, but you couldn't earn a living that way. And besides, in the mid-twenties, talkies were just a gleam in the eye of some crazy inventor.

This time I found three possible marks. The first was by the word "dazzling," a term I thought appropriate to the Velazquez emerald, by all accounts. "Lucille Thornbush" seemed to have been faintly underlined in the sentence, "Miss Lucille Thornbush contributes hilarity as Daphne's maid Delilah." Finally, I thought I detected a spidery stroke under the word "wine." The dialogue, "Your lips are like wine and I would drink from them forevermore," was being roundly and justifiably ridiculed by the reviewer. "Wine," of course, suggested champagne, but what the hell did that mean? Did Betty own a share in a French winery, from which she shipped surreptitious presents to her daughter? Or did she mean to indicate that she had bankrolled a bootleg operation during Prohibition, and secreted the profits on part of the Roman Empire set for *The Beautiful Martyr*? Or that she had drunk her fortune away?

When I finished the review, I glanced up at the credits to see whose script was under attack and found the name of P. C. Stinger. This name rang a bell, so I looked up the scriptwriters on the other two films. P. C. Stinger again. Was it unusual in those days for a writer to write several scripts for one actress? I decided to ask old Stephen "Morning Star" Grunewald. While I was at it, I noticed that the same director, James Young, made two of the three films. I decided to ask Grunewald about him, too. All this case needed was another suspect or two.

"Anybody named Harrison," said Kevin later that evening, "who goes by the whole thing, and not Harry or Sonny or something, I put at the top of my list of suspects on principle." He was cracking pecans at his kitchen table, and Sadie's ears jumped at every crack. I don't know why she put up with him. I don't know why he couldn't go to the store and buy pecans in one of those little plastic bags like everybody else.

"Yeah, but what about Edgar P. Kirkendahl? Doesn't 'Edgar' strike you as just a tad nefarious, or am I being too literary?"

"You don't know what his wife calls him," Kevin pointed out reasonably. "Maybe she calls him Ed, or Eddie, or Gary, or Pops. But Harrison's wife calls him Harrison. That seems to me significant."

"Point taken. But somehow it doesn't seem very scientific to eliminate Bill McGann and Stephen Grunewald on the basis of their first names. Or Harold Waite, who really does seem to go by Harry."

He shrugged. "Okay, so who's *your* favorite suspect?"

"Harrison or Edgar or Harold," I admitted. "They're all bastards, in different ways. My vote goes to Harrison, not for his name, but because he's an arrogant son of a bitch who's also a gynecologist, and I'd love to see one of those guys made to suffer for their numerous crimes. Edgar Kirkendahl is a capitalist pig, rich enough not to worry about his public image, which immediately makes me suspicious. Harold Waite is a condescending bastard, full of fake good humor. But if we're talking arrogance and self-importance, Grunewald runs them a close fourth. And who knows? Bill McGann's unprepossessing exterior may be a clever ruse intended to disguise the egomaniacal tendencies often evident in passionate politicos. Look at Eddie Haskell."

"I didn't know he was involved in politics."

"It's the type I'm discussing. My son Jason had a friend just like him once. A weasel in sheep's clothing. So goddamned polite you couldn't be rude to him. Chief instigator of every dangerous, illegal, or downright dopey scheme my son ever got involved in. And I don't mean to let my own offspring off the hook; he just didn't have the brains or imagination to think up the kind of stuff I'm talking about. Now his friend is representing the third district, God love 'em."

"Do we know if any of these guys know Waite?"

"I checked membership directories for the Cincinnati Club and the Queen City Club."

"Your own?" he asked incredulously.

"Are you kidding? The fucking Queen City Club doesn't even allow persons of my gender above the first floor. I just happen to be well connected, is all. Anyway, Waite and Kirkendahl are both members of both clubs. Grunewald and Prescott don't belong, and neither, needless to say, does McGann."

"Have you eliminated the St. Francis crowd from consideration?"

I got hit between the eyes by flying pecan shrapnel and gave him a look. "No, not entirely. I mean, they're really the most logical suspects because they were closest to the two victims. Landau says most of them have alibis of sorts for one or the other of the murders, although some of those alibis rely on the confirmation of one other person. Curtis and Obie don't have anything definite for the Saturday Betty was killed, but they were down at the Drop In Center playing poker the night Lucille died. There were three other guys in the game willing to swear that they never left for longer than it took to go to the john. On the Saturday when Betty was killed, Trish was down at SPU working on a mailing. Bill McGann alibis her for at least part of the time, but since he left for a while — he says for lunch at a hot dog stand on Fountain Square — neither of them is really in the clear. Jinks, who was with Betty when she bought the knife, doesn't remember where he was on any of these occasions, but maintains that he was probably panhandling down by the stadium on Saturday around noon. Steel says it's none of the cops' goddamn business where he was, and they should go ahead and arrest him if they think they have something on him. Patty says she was with Zona both times, and Zona says it's true. But since Zona never leaves Never-Never Land, who knows where they really were."

"What do the cops say about alibis for the others?"

"You mean Eddie and Harry and Harry and Billy and Stevie? They don't, except for Billy and Harry Waite. Harry was supposed to have been in Florida on the day Betty was killed, taking his boat out for a test run. It sounds like such a trumped-up alibi, so I could be persuaded to give it to him on that basis alone. The night Lucille was killed he was — guess where? — at the movies with his perky young secretary. The rest aren't seen as being closely enough connected to Betty or Lucille to be suspects."

"So where does that leave you?"

"Damned if I know. I haven't even factored in any ex-husbands or lovers. But I do have my secret weapon."

"Which is?" He bounced a shell fragment off my chin.

"Leon. Leon Jakes is my secret weapon."

CHAPTER 18

The next day I spent the morning on the phone. First, I tracked down Grunewald, no small feat since school was due to start again in three weeks, and the faculty generally seizes this last opportunity to hole up in the library or rent a houseboat in Michigan. Luckily, I found someone who knew that Grunewald had rented a cottage on Cape Cod, and who knew someone who knew someone with the phone number. Obviously, the police hadn't delivered one of their warnings about not leaving town. Nor did he seem to have the kind of guilty conscience that kept him awake nights as long as Cat Caliban and Cincinnati's Finest were still on the case.

Sitting in front of a fan that was blowing muggy air in my face, I asked him about P. C. Stinger and James Young.

"Young's dead. Died a long time ago. Yes, he did make several films with Leda Marrs for Vitagraph, but as I say, you'll find it difficult to question him about them. Unfortunately, he died when my research was in the early stages, so I wasn't able to speak to him either. Now, Phyl Stinger is another matter. She must be pushing ninety. She was perfectly lucid when I talked to her, but cantankerous. Wouldn't talk to me at first, and when she did, wouldn't say much without Leda's authorization, which Leda wasn't interested in giving. But I had the impression they'd been good friends, and perhaps still were."

"How can I get in touch with her?"

"She lives somewhere around here, actually — the Cape, I mean. Let me think. Not Provincetown. Wellfleet? No, I just don't remember. If I were at home, I could look it up, but I don't have it with me."

"Is she in a nursing home?"

"No, she's got her own place — or did. She could be gaga by now." He said this with a satisfied air, as if it would serve her right for past cantankerousness.

"So my best bet would be calling information for every town on Cape Cod to ask for a Phyl Stinger?"

"Phyllis is her name — or P.C. But they're all in the same area code, so it won't matter as long as you get an operator who's willing to be helpful. I wish I could help, but as I explained earlier, I'm devoting my energies, including my mental energies, to D. W. Griffith these days. The Leda Marrs materials are ancient history."

"Yeah, I understand. I wonder, though—" I'd been debating with myself about this part. How much of my hand was I willing to give away in the interest of getting him to reveal his?

"Yes?"

"Is there anything special I should know about Betty's connection to Rome, or Romans, or about the Roman set from her first picture, *The Beautiful Martyr*?"

There was a silence on the other end. Either he was overwhelmed by the excitement of having an important clue dropped in his lap, or he was speculating on the likelihood that I was cuckoo.

"Why do you ask?"

"It's just something that came up in a conversation I had with somebody the other day, I can't tell you who, since they asked to remain anonymous." I lied with the practiced glibness of a mother of three.

"Rome, huh? To tell you the truth, I can't think of a thing. She did have an Italian admirer for a while, but I don't know if he was from Rome. Now what was his name? I don't think I put it in the book. I would have had to make a separate appendix just to list the names of all the men she ran around with. What *was* that fellow's name? No, sorry, I'm not going to remember it."

"But that's the only association you remember with Rome or Romans?"

"Yes, but I'll give it some thought if you like. Perhaps something will come to me."

"Good. I'd appreciate that."

I hung up and dialed information for Cape Cod, wondering if he was on the phone to Phyl now, warning her about me. Maybe he knew her better than he let on. Maybe they were secretly colluding to find Betty's emerald. The operator took no time at all in locating a P. C. Stinger in Truro. I dialed.

You know how some people answer the phone as if they were very, very busy, and already late for a meeting with Donald Trump? That's how this voice sounded, and it didn't improve when it identified itself as Phyllis Stinger. I blew my cool and said something really tacky.

"Ms. Stinger, I'm a private investigator looking into the death of Betty Grumbacher, whose stage name was—"

"The *what?*"

"The death of Betty Grumbacher."

"What in holy hell happened to Betty? She's eight years younger than I am, for chrissake." It was the deep, raspy voice of a hardened smoker, and I could hear her let out a puff at the end of this comment.

"I'm sorry. I forgot that you might not have heard about her — death." That's me. As soon as I've been really gauche, I come all over discretion.

"What'd she die of?"

"She was murdered."

"Shit. Goddamn it." I could hear her stabbing at the ashtray. "How's Lucille taking it?"

"Lucille?" I suddenly wished I had that service where your phone beeps and you have to put the person you're talking to on hold. Where's Ma Bell when you need her? "Uh, Lucille died."

"*Lucille* died? Lucille *Shelton*? What the hell did *she* die of?"

"Uh — she was murdered, too. I'm sort of investigating both murders at the same time. I think they're connected."

"Well, Christ, unless you got a psychopath on the loose in Sin City, it sure as hell sounds like it. How'd they get killed?"

So I told her the whole story. She listened in silence. Then she let loose a chain of expletives that made me sound like Rebecca of Sunnybrook Farm. I have my limits, after all, though you might not think it. But she was a writer, and she'd developed her God-given talent into high art. She was a master manipulator of the English language as recorded in the *Dictionary of Slang*.

Then she began to ask questions. Had Betty been robbed? Sexually assaulted? If she'd been searched, did I think the killer had found anything? Was I *sure* there wasn't anything else in the safe deposit box? Had Lucille left anything at her cousin's place? Had I looked through her effects?

"What am I looking for? That's what I'd like to know. That's why I called you — on a hunch that you might know something about her estate."

"Not really. I guess Lucille was the executor."

"That's right."

"And the cops searched Betty's place?"

"She didn't have a place. She was living on the streets."

"What? That's bullshit. Of course, she had a place. I used to send mail there. What the hell would she be doing on the streets?"

"Do you have the address?" I thought I knew what was coming, but I asked anyway.

"Sure, hang on. Gotta find my little black book. That's the right color for it anyway. When you get to be my age, you cross out more names than you write in. How old are you?"

"Fifty-nine."

She snorted. "Goddamn teenybopper. Here it is. 1407 Sycamore, apartment 403."

"You got the same address for Lucille?"

"Well, I sent her Christmas cards care of Betty."

"The apartment on Sycamore belongs to Lucille's cousin. They were both on the streets when they died. Had been for years."

"Hell. Goddamn it to hell. What were they doing on the streets, for chrissake?"

"Everybody says it's because they didn't have rent money," I said cautiously.

She snorted again. "*Rent* money? Christ, Betty could've bought a goddamn *apartment complex* and had plenty left over." She was quiet a minute. "I get it. Where's the dough? That's what everybody's looking for, isn't it? You want to know where all her money is if it's not where anybody can find it. And you think she was killed for it, is that it?"

"That's one possibility. But you're the first person I've talked to who thinks Betty had anything left. Everybody else seems to think she spent everything she had on her mother's medical bills and her own."

"Jesus, she could have bought the Mayo Clinic if she'd cashed in that rock of hers. Not that she would've parted with it. But there was plenty more."

"You mean gifts she received during the twenties?"

"Well, there was plenty of loot there, I can tell you. And lots of flaming assholes to say Betty lived extravagantly and left Hollywood in rags, but that's all crap. Betty liked a good time, I'm not saying she didn't, and she gave a hell of a party, but she was too smart to part with the whole enchilada. And then I got the impression there'd been more since."

"More what?"

"Tokens of affection, I think they're called."

I was stunned. This angle had never occurred to me. "Tokens of *whose* affection?"

"Well, I don't know that I should say," she mused, blowing smoke into my ear.

"Ms. Stinger, we're talking murder here."

"Right. Call me Phyl. Well, hell, you can probably guess anyway."

"The sheik?" I felt like I was on a goddamn soap opera.

I suspected she was nodding into the phone. "I don't know what he sent, but he was a romantic son of a bitch, I'll give him that. And he never shopped a bargain basement in his life."

"So you think she still had the emerald and that he sent her other presents over the years? Wasn't he married?"

"Oh, hell, yes. But those Middle Eastern types never let that stop them carrying a torch. And that's what it was, you know. Just another man in love with his youth. Christ, I bet he never would've recognized Betty twenty years afterward, and who knows if she would've recognized him? Of course, his picture was in the papers more than hers later on, so she might have."

"But you're saying you don't think they met?"

"Shit, no. That would've spoiled the romance. But what I don't get is why she lived on the streets. Like I say, she had more than enough to live comfortably with plenty left over. And besides, you say Lucille was on the streets, too. It wouldn't be like Betty to be stingy like that. She and Lucille were like sisters. Why wouldn't she give Lucille enough to pay rent somewhere?"

"Maybe because she didn't think of the money as hers. Maybe she had a closer relative in mind than her sister."

"Her daughter, you mean? Yeah, I guess that makes sense, in a screwy kind of way. Betty was always nuts about that kid. She didn't want to give up the baby — that was her mother's idea. She took the kid home to show off to Mother, and came back without it. Said her mother had convinced her that Hollywood was no place to raise a kid. If you ask me, her mother was a first-class bitch who ran her daughter's life, even long distance. Movies were her mother's idea and she didn't want anything to get in the way of her daughter's career. As it turned out, her career didn't last much longer anyway, and I always thought she regretted not keeping the baby after things went sour. Maybe that's why she ended up in the bughouse so often. It wasn't just booze and pills and being washed up; it was what she gave up and what she got in return that really killed her. Yeah, come to think of it, I can see Betty living out her life like one of my worst scripts — living on the streets, refusing to spend a penny on herself. Then one day she'd die and the world would be stunned by the fortune she left behind. And her daughter would realize how much her mother really loved her. Solid gold horseshit, but it would play big at the box office."

"Do you know if she ever saw her daughter after she gave her up for adoption?"

"Yeah, she'd take the bus out to the suburbs where the kid lived and kind of hang around watching for her. Not often, you understand, but I think she did it a couple of times. Said the kid looked like her father — is that true? You seen her?"

"Yes. She looks Arabic, I can say that."

"How'd she take Betty's death?"

"Pretty calmly. Mostly puzzled. She didn't know who her mother was, never thought much about it, she says. She seemed sad that Betty needed help and she didn't know about it, but she can't really grieve for someone she never met."

"Is the kid nice?"

"Well, she's hardly a kid anymore, except by your standards. She's okay. I didn't feel one way or the other about her, though I wanted to like her. She doesn't need Betty's money, if appearances can be trusted."

"Looks can be deceiving. It's the bastards that have everything that talk themselves into needing more. What about Lucille? You think the killer was looking for something, say the emerald, and went after Lucille because he thought she knew where it was?"

"That's one theory."

"Poor Lucille. She would've stood her ground, too, God love her. She was quieter than Betty, but she had a backbone of steel. Had to, to be a Black actress in Hollywood in those days. Shit, any days."

"Listen, I really appreciate your talking to me. Can I call you again if I need something?"

"Sure, why not? I'm holed up here until the goddamn tourist season is over. Writing my goddamn memoirs."

I hung up. Ninety. It gave a body pause. Made me think I should be out doing roadwork with V.I. and Kinsey.

CHAPTER 19

At two o'clock Mel came home. She'd been throwing pots, she said, and it looked like she'd been throwing them at somebody and they'd retaliated. Two cats circled her ankles, sniffing. She brought me a book on "Black Hollywood" that she'd checked out of the public library. Lucille Thornbush Shelton was on page sixty-four. She pointed a grubby finger at Lucille's photograph.

"That's a picture of Lucille from 1924. I looked it up in the list of illustrations."

Lucille was a light-skinned variation on her cousin Sophronia, slender with delicate features. Her hair was cut short and bobbed. She was dressed in a dropped-waist flowered number from the twenties, with a fringed shawl draped around her shoulders, and she was gazing up at a good-looking young man.

"Is this a film she made?" I was surprised. No bandana.

"Independent production by a 'colored' company. White money invested in Black entertainment. Called *Ebony Enchantment*, something like that."

"I guess there wasn't enough work in these kinds of productions for her to make a living in Hollywood."

Mel shook her head. "They made for a nice change for actresses like Louise Beavers, who mostly appeared padded and kerchiefed in mainstream films. Actors got to make a whole film without saying 'honey chile' once. It supplemented their incomes as busboys and motel maids, but it didn't earn their keep."

"Shit, look at that face. Doesn't it piss you off to know what happened to her?"

I spent the rest of the afternoon in my property owner's hat, trying to change a goddamn toilet seat. Sometimes even we detectives have to do this kind of thing. If you have attempted this operation yourself, you'll know what my afternoon was like. If you haven't, words can't describe it. Sidney sat on the tank and watched, and once he was so startled by a flying expletive, he nearly fell in. When he grows up, he'll think back fondly on these times we spent together, mother and son. His sisters were off snoozing somewhere cooler and quieter. They are not victims of gendered socialization; they had been in on quite a few of my home repair projects over the years, and they knew what to expect. It was six o'clock when I threw in the towel and called a plumber. That's why they make so much money, plumbers — they charge you for your time as well as their own.

I had promised to go shopping with Mabel that evening.

Mabel's water ballet class had a recital coming up, and she had some kind of featured role — I think maybe she bobbed up in the middle of the circle. Anyway, I'd promised to go swimsuit shopping with her. Now, going with Mabel to try on bathing suits is roughly equivalent to taking Nancy Reagan curtain shopping at Odd Lots: it is an enterprise doomed to failure. But lest my children use this as evidence against me in a commitment hearing someday, I want to go on record as pointing out that Mabel is my dear friend and I would do anything for her, even though she can be a pain in the ass. Plus, Northgate Mall is air conditioned.

Like I say, the cards were stacked against us. First off, this was August, the month after the swimsuit sale, when they move what's left into the "resort attire" section and jack up the price twenty percent so they can fill the racks with Pendleton wool and corduroy. Mabel decided she should try on those suits cut up the side to that little dip in the cellulite where your waist is supposed to be. She read somewhere that they were slimming. After hours in the dressing room, poor Mabel was ready to weep with frustration, so I took her to Graeter's for a double dip of mocha chip. My heart went out to her. She wanted a suit that made her look like Esther Williams in *Million Dollar Mermaid*, and it didn't exist. I dropped Mabel off and headed home.

In fact, I was thinking about Esther Williams when I turned the corner onto my street, so I didn't notice the flashing blue lights right at first. When I did notice them, I wondered what house was having a domestic disturbance. When I noticed they were parked in front of the Catatonia Arms, I felt a little cold-footed mouse scamper up my spine. First, I got scared. Then I got mad. If somebody'd left me another goddamn corpse, I'd sue the son of a bitch for damaging my reputation and my business.

The neighbors were lined up watching the sideshow. There was a guy sitting in the back of one of the three blue-and-whites behind the grating, but I couldn't see him too well. There were two cops hanging out on the front lawn, shooting the bull and occasionally mumbling into their walkie-talkies. My apartment was all lit up, and I could see another cop in the hallway.

"You guys having a union meeting on my front lawn or is there something going on I should know about?"

Somebody brushed past me with a video camera that had "Channel 12" on the side.

"You live here?" Cop Number 1 said.

"I own the joint."

"Mrs. Calabash, right?" Cop Number 2 said.

"Caliban."

"Where you been, Mrs. Caliban? We been looking for you."

"Do I get to know what for or is that a state secret?"

"No secret. You had a break-in."

"That the guy that did it?" I nodded at the squad car.

"Yep. That's him, all right."

Somebody else pushed past us, muttering "Press" and flashing an ID.

"So how come I'm on the national news?"

Cop Number 1 grinned. "Your cats caught him. Your cats and your neighbor. Your cats are heroes."

Upstairs at Mel and Al's, there was a press conference in progress. Sadie and Sophie were nowhere in sight. Considering all the commotion, I figured they were hiding in a closet somewhere. I elbowed my way through the crowd, and there, sitting in the middle of the kitchen table, was Sidney. He was cuddling up to Kit Andrews from Channel 12 and purring into her mike. That's my boy.

"Mrs. C, isn't he something?" Kevin was nudging me in the forearm.

"What are you doing here? You're supposed to be at work."

"And miss all the excitement? No way."

"I called him," Mel confessed. "I knew he'd never forgive me if I didn't."

"Hey," somebody said behind me. "You the lady that owns the pussycat?"

"I live with him." I eyed Sidney, who was now sprawled shamelessly across the table, playing with the dangles on Norma Rashid's bracelets and batting his baby yellows at a photographer from the *Enquirer.*

"Would you say he's an especially intelligent cat?"

"I'd say he knows who belongs in his house and who doesn't."

"Is he trained?"

"Cats don't need training. They take to their litter boxes like ducks to water."

"No, uh, I meant, is he trained to watch for strangers?"

I thought of Sidney practicing his technique from the front flower beds.

"No, it comes naturally. He watches lots of nature shows on television."

"How old is he?"

"Older than he looks." He had his teeth sunk in somebody's light meter.

"About these other two cats — uh, Stacey and—"

"Sadie."

"Stacey and Sadie."

"No, Sadie and Sophie."

"Do they often work as a team? All three, I mean?"

"Only in the hours before dinner and breakfast."

"What do you feed them?"

"Cat food."

The guy with the light meter was holding it overhead and Sidney was leaping for the dangling strap.

"No, I mean, what kind? Our readers love that human interest stuff."

"Tuna. He's a tuna junkie."

"He eats pizza at my house," Kevin put in.

"No kidding? With anchovies?"

"No, he doesn't like anchovies."

"What?" This from the usually reticent Mel. "He loves anchovies. He eats them all the time up here."

"Well, he won't eat them at my place." They turned to me to settle the dispute.

"Don't look at me. I never let an anchovy cross my threshold."

"Listen, Mrs. Calabash—"

"Caliban."

"Oh, Caliban. First name?"

"Catherine." I silenced Kevin with a look.

"Mrs. Caliban, don't you think we could get a shot of you with all three cats?"

"I doubt it. I think the others have moved in with the people across the street."

"Well, then, one of you and Sidney."

"I don't think so."

"Oh, come on, Mrs. C. Your grandchildren will love it."

Kevin was shoving me forward.

"Yeah, and my children will change their names." Someone pushed Sidney into my arms, where he wriggled happily and looked up at me for signs of approval. His attack cat routine had paid off in spades. I was too busy glaring at Kevin to praise Sidney. When the picture appeared in the papers, I looked like I had constipation.

It was some time later before I found out what had happened while I was watching Mabel imitate a contortionist in the dressing room at McAlpin's. Al had been out to a meeting, and Mel was home watching a "Cagney and Lacey" rerun. The door to the hall was open. She heard a funny noise and glanced up to discover Sadie standing in the doorway. She assumed Sadie wanted to come in and visit. A few minutes passed, and then Sadie came into the room, stood in front of the television, and yowled. Mel told her she was watching "Cagney and Lacey" and could Sadie please keep it down until the next commercial. Sadie disappeared for a minute or two, then returned to yowl again. Mel was struck by the sound, since it wasn't from her familiar repertoire. Also, Sadie was staring at her. Mercifully, a commercial came on and Mel stood up. Sadie bolted for the door, looking behind her to make sure Mel would follow. She paused on the landing, hunkered down the way cats do when they're waiting for something to happen, and peered down the stairs. Mel realized then that Sophie was crouched on the stairs, about halfway down, in the same attitude, both noses pointed toward my door. She heard a noise coming from my apartment and barely had time to say, "What the hell's going on down there?" when a man emerged, screaming, wearing Sidney for a hat. The man danced around in the hallway, slapping at Sidney, who was holding on for dear life and drawing more blood than a dental hygienist. This gave Mel time to vault down the stairs, give a few blood-curdling karate shouts (or whatever they call them in her branch of martial arts) and deck the poor bastard. Sidney let go of his scalp and retreated a pace, only to take a few more swipes at his adversary, even though the guy was out cold. Mel had to drag him off, hissing and spitting, and explain to him about the code of honor. He didn't take it very well, but Sadie and Sophie consoled him by licking the blood off of him. It was all, Mel assured me, the burglar's blood.

What can I say? His goddamn male hormones kicked in and he defended his turf.

CHAPTER 20

The suspect, as I knew I was supposed to regard him, hadn't done much damage before Sidney had nailed him. He'd carried my boom box to the front door along with a couple pieces of jewelry he'd found, but he hadn't messed with the TV. No, where he'd really concentrated his efforts was my office. The desk lamp was on and he'd pulled out the desk drawers and started rummaging. Both the rent receipt book and *The Landlord's Handbook* were speckled with blood, so I guess this was where he'd been sitting when Sidney sprang from the top of the file cabinet behind him. The desk seemed a funny place to look for fenceable merchandise; you didn't need to be a goddamn genius to guess he was looking for something else altogether. To tell you the truth, it tickled me to think somebody regarded me as dangerous enough to send a thug around to search my desk, even a second-rate thug. And it was only my first case.

Sidney sauntered in and jumped up on the desk, all prepared to re-enact his moment of glory for my benefit. So I petted him and fussed over him and called him names I won't reprint here for fear of embarrassing us both.

I didn't think the suspect had gotten away with anything. All the valuable stuff I had collected so far was filed away in the apartment files under Number Three. After all, that was where the corpse had shown up, so it seemed logical to me. But I doubted it would to anyone else.

What had the guy come looking for? The photocopies of the contents of Betty's safe deposit box? The articles on Transstar Associates? Or something else I didn't have? Did they just want to check my notes on the case to see what I knew? Or did they think I had a treasure map, with "X Marks the Spot" over the location of Betty's emerald necklace? Or maybe they were looking for something to blackmail me with if I got too close. Dream on, fellas. Pure as the goddamned driven snow: that's me.

Mel and I went down to the station in the morning to sign off on a shitload of paperwork. Robbery passed me on to Homicide.

"His name is Richie Heinrich," Fricke said, eyeing us as if we were reluctant to acknowledge an illegitimate brother. "Name mean anything?"

"Nope. Does he have an arrest record?"

"Hell, he's got a record as long as your arm." This from my old pal, Eddie Landau. "Mostly breaking and entering, burglary, stuff like that."

"Was he armed?"

"Is the Pope Catholic?"

"What happened to his piece?" I was really getting into this. They exchanged a look.

"Your cat disarmed him. The weapon's in police custody."

I nodded. "Sidney hates firearms. They make a loud noise."

"Yeah, how come you didn't bring Sidney in for a lineup?" Mel wanted to know.

Fricke shot her a glance. He didn't know if she was kidding or not.

"I guess you know he was looking for something," I said.

"Burglars usually are," Fricke said cautiously.

"In a desk drawer? Is that where burglars usually start looking? I've got a lot to learn."

"Okay, so he wasn't after the family silver. What was he looking for in the desk drawer?"

"Search me." Landau was fidgeting, so I didn't meet his eye.

"I heard a rumor — correct me if I'm wrong — I heard a rumor that you been sticking your nose in police business, running around interviewing people about the Grumbacher murder."

"You'd be surprised how much you learn that way."

"For instance?"

"Some folks think Betty still owned an emerald as big as your bald spot."

"I guess that's why she was on the streets. Good disguise for a millionairess."

"Some folks think she was saving it for her daughter. Some folks think that will is worth a lot of money."

He was studying me. "Yeah? I suppose you know where this emerald is hiding."

"Some folks might think I do. Then again, some folks might think I know why Betty was collecting articles on the real estate dealings of Transstar Associates."

He grunted. "Transstar Associates? Who the hell are they?"

"A real estate investment firm Betty was looking into."

"And I suppose you know why Grumbacher was doing that?"

"Some folks might think I do."

"Goddamn it! This ain't no game of Monopoly! This is murder we're talking about, Caliban!" He had turned a dangerous color of red, and I was mentally reviewing my CPR training. "If you got *relevant* information, and I mean *relevant*, you'd better hand it over, and butt the hell out! Your cat may have saved your ass this time, but they might send a smarter thug next time."

"You mean, one armed with catnip?" This was Mel, disingenuous.

Fricke stalked over and kicked a file cabinet. I turned to Landau.

"You know, he has a point. This Heinrich guy can't be too bright. Who would pick him to do their dirty work? One look at his arrest record and you'd know it was long odds he wouldn't be caught. Would *you* hire a mug who's on a first-name basis with the Workhouse cook?"

"Maybe we're dealing with someone who doesn't know a lot of local hoodlums."

"Yeah, I guess you can't advertise under 'Breaking and Entering' in the *Wheeler Dealer.*"

Fricke completed his circuit limping.

"Have you got any information for me, Caliban? Yes or no."

"Christ, I gave you everything I got, what do you want from me? I could've pointed out that it was all stuff you should've got for yourself, but no. I'm too big a person to do that."

Fricke shuffled to the door and opened it, a little vein jumping up and down on his temple like a performing flea. I swept out in what I hoped looked like righteous indignation, tipping Eddie a wink as I passed. Mel stomped out behind me. "If that broad ever applies for a P.I. license in this state . . ." I heard as the door shut.

"Who's he think he's fooling? The way he runs an investigation, I'll be retired five years before he ever finds out I was in business."

We stepped outside and clapped on our shades.

"If he'd been civil to me, I would've given him Leon Jakes. But he had to spoil it all by being an arrogant, self-righteous son of a bitch. What you want to bet he doesn't even know there's a witness who probably saw Betty's murderer? Not that I think Richie did it. He probably would have tripped on his shoelaces on his way out the door and we would have found him out cold at the foot of the stairs. Still, in the interest of thoroughness, they ought to call Leon down for a lineup."

"Where to, boss?" Mel slid behind the wheel of her red Celica.

"Your roomie work around here?"

"Sure, couple blocks away."

"Let's go visit."

The difference between the offices of a prestigious Cincinnati law firm and the Legal Aid Society was like the difference between Cartier's and K-Mart. It was partitioned to give some semblance of privacy, but you could hear the buzz of voices and the ringing of telephones as soon as you walked in the door.

"Hi, kids! How'd it go?" Al poked her head around a partition in the far corner when the secretary buzzed her. "So to what do I owe the honor? You want me to file charges of police brutality?"

That gave me pause, but Mel caught the glint in my eye and said firmly, "No, we don't."

"The guy we identified is named Richie Heinrich. He's got quite a record in petty theft. Do you think you can dig up any information on him? I mean is there any way to tell who his associates are?"

"Well, I might be able to tell you who he got arrested or tried with, if that's what you mean. But that's assuming he's not a solo operator. As for trial records, he may never have gone to court. He may have plea bargained every conviction."

"Can you tell me whether he's ever broken into any other offices I'm interested in — say, SPU or Kirkendahl's? Or whether Waite ever represented him? I don't suppose there's an easy way to link him with a gynecologist or a college professor, unless he's a college dropout who had a sex change, but can you check into his background?"

"Sure. I'll see what I can do. It may take me a while, though, and I'm due in court tomorrow."

We stopped at the courthouse on the way home to check the county marriage records. It had occurred to me that I shouldn't trust Grunewald. Even if he wasn't a murderer, he might be a sloppy researcher, though I doubted it. We looked up a few other things while we were at it, like Mildred Grumbacher's will. All in all, you could say the highlight of the day was lunch at Izzy Kadetz's deli.

At home on the kitchen table I found a note in what looked to be the handwriting of a sleepy three-year-old — Kevin's. "Call Al," it said. Next to it was a smallish cardboard box tied up with string. I untied it and looked inside. There, lying on a bed of tissue paper was a gun. The note on top, in the same wobbly handwriting, said, "Call for instructions before use."

I was scared to touch the thing. On the barrel, it said, "S. & W. 38 Special." There was some kind of logo above the handle, and above the trigger, it said, "Made in U.S.A." Well, at least it was American made; that was a comfort. Wedged in the corner was a box of cartridges. It said, "WARNING, Keep out of the reach of children." Nothing about grandmothers.

I padded across the hall and banged on Kevin's door, but he was out. I heard him in the hall about an hour later and opened my door.

"Who'm I supposed to call?"

"Me."

"Aw, hell, you've been holding out on me. I thought you were going to take shooting lessons with me."

"I will. What I know about guns is a bartender's knowledge. If somebody points one at me, I duck. But I guess I know the basics."

"Wait. Where'd this gun come from anyway?" I was growing suspicious.

"From the Lost and Found at work."

"Meaning you took it off somebody."

Kevin shrugged. "He lost it and I found it. It was in his hand at the time. It's a little surcharge we add when folks get drunk and pistol happy."

"So it's registered to this guy?"

"I doubt it. If it were, he might have come back to claim it."

"So it's unregistered? You gave me an unregistered gun?"

"Look. Mrs. C. Do me a favor. If you're cornered by a dangerous criminal with a gun, don't stop to worry whether he's gonna ask to see your registration. You're welcome to register it if you want to. Tell 'em you found it in a box of embroidered pillowcases you picked up at an auction."

"But I don't know anything about guns." He picked it up and I ducked.

"This here is the front part, where the bullets come out. If you want to fire at somebody, point this part at them. It's called the barrel. Don't point it at anything you're unwilling to put a hole in, even if you don't think it's loaded. If you just want to scare the shit out of somebody, point it down and look mean. This here is the back part, where you hold on. It's called the butt. You use it to conk people over the head with. Often more effective than shooting them if you want to stop them dead in their tracks, so to speak. This little doohickey here is where your index finger goes when you're ready to fire. It's called the trigger. The bullets go in this round thingamajigger, called the cylinder, just the way you've seen the sheriff do it in TV Westerns. The cylinder makes this gun a revolver, for reasons you can probably guess. If you get in a tight spot, and you don't think you can bluff your way out by just waving it around, just squeeze the trigger, good and hard. To sight your target, look down the barrel here until this front blade lines up with the notch here on the back. Focus on the sights, not the target. Oh, and did I tell you to use both hands?"

"I don't know," I said dubiously. "I got more instructions than this on my washing machine. You mean if I pull the trigger it'll fire without my cocking it?"

"Right. It's called double action. Got it?" He handed it to me.

I held it at arm's length, leaning away, and pointed it at the refrigerator. Then I thought better of endangering a major appliance out of warranty and pointed it at the floor.

"Couldn't I just carry an umbrella?"

"Hardened criminals have no respect for umbrellas. Trust me on this. And it's more portable than a cat. With any luck, you won't have to use it at all. But if you're going to be a private investigator, you're going to have to get used to carrying a gun. And after last night, the sooner the better."

"Oh, hell, that poor bastard would probably have shot his foot off if he'd tried to fire at something."

"Maybe so. But better safe than sorry."

This philosophy had something to recommend it. However, it seemed to me I'd always heard that guns were dangerous because the person carrying one got disarmed and shot with it. I thought of poor Betty and her knife and shivered. Maybe I wouldn't put any bullets in it. That way I could still scare people with it and conk them over the head, but at least I wouldn't get shot by my own gun.

I put the gun down in its box and went and called Al.

"Looks like you were right, Cat. I haven't finished checking Heinrich, but it didn't take long to find out something interesting. Guess who his attorney was seven years ago?"

"Harold Waite."

"You got it."

CHAPTER 21

It was nice to be right about something, I admit it. But where did it get me? After all, I couldn't even be sure that the person who arranged the burglary and the person who murdered Betty and Lucille were one and the same. And as Al said, she hadn't finished checking. Maybe Richie knew every goddamn suspect I had. In the past, when I'd wanted to know who spilled grape juice on the sofa, the cast of suspects was limited, however the suspects themselves tried to suggest otherwise. If only I could line them all up and have Leon take a look at them.

It turned out somebody else had the same idea. That night I received a call from Helen Prescott.

"Mrs. Caliban? This is Helen Prescott, Betty Grumbacher's daughter. I'm calling to let you know about a local memorial service for my mother that's going to be held next Saturday at Christ Church down on 4th Street at eight o'clock. It's being sponsored by the local chapter of the Screen Actors Guild. I thought you might like to know about it since you seemed so interested in my mother."

That was putting it mildly.

"What a nice idea!" I enthused, coming all over grandmotherly. "How did this come about?"

"Oh, well, you know, Harrison and I had talked so much about Mother, and he could see I was upset about her death. And after I read the book, and saw how famous she'd been and all, it seemed sad that nobody really knew about her — I mean, knew that Leda Marrs had died. So Harrison said perhaps the Screen Actors Guild would like to sponsor a memorial service and use it to publicize their fund for indigent actors. Well, I thought it was a lovely idea, and the people at the local chapter liked it, too, so there we were."

"I didn't know there was a local chapter."

"I don't suppose I did, either, but Harrison says all those people who make commercials are members, so of course there would have to be one."

"So this was all Dr. Prescott's idea?"

"Well, actually, I think it came up in a conversation he had with Mother's attorney, Mr. Waite. He can't really remember who thought of it first, but he and Mr. Waite are both helping to organize it. And Mr. Grunewald, the author of the book, you know, he's going to come and speak about Leda Marrs's career."

"That will be nice. Are any of the Street People United folks involved?"

She hesitated. "I believe someone contacted a man there, but they said he didn't seem very enthusiastic or helpful. I don't know why."

I did. They'd already held their own service of sorts, and McGann was probably offended that the Screen Actors Guild was going to cash in on Betty's death and leave SPU out in the cold. Unless he didn't want to be seen in public where he might be associated with Betty's death.

"Mr. Grunewald has been so helpful. He's helped us to track down a number of people who knew Mother in the old days."

"Is Phyl Stinger one of them?"

"Oh, is she a writer? Yes, I think she's coming." Curiouser and curiouser. If only they could manage to bring in Kirkendahl, we'd have a full house.

"Did you ask SPU to advertise the service, even if they didn't want to be officially represented?"

"You know, I'll have to check with Harrison. I think he was the one who talked to them. I don't know if he thought to ask or not."

"Do you mind if I ask you something?"

"No, of course not."

"Did you mention to the Screen Actors Guild that another actress had died two weeks after your mother did?"

"I didn't know. Who was that? Oh, you mean the Black lady? Was she an actress, too?"

"Her name was Lucille Thornbush and she appeared in about fifteen films, some of them your mother's. Leda Marrs may have been more famous, but Lucille Thornbush has an equal claim to the Screen Actors Guild's attention." I was trying not to sound pissed off. It wouldn't have accomplished what I wanted to accomplish, and anyway, half the writers of film reference books didn't seem to know shit about Lucille, so why should Helen Prescott? I had another theory about why Bill McGann felt the way he did about this upscale memorial service. "She was your mother's best friend. Betty would have wanted them to be honored equally."

"Oh, of course. I absolutely agree. Why, I feel terribly about the oversight, and of course I'll speak to Harrison about it immediately. I'm sure they'll all want to include — oh, dear, what did you say her name was?"

"Lucille Thornbush Shelton."

"Yes, I'm sure they'll want to include Mrs. Shelton in the service."

I thanked her for calling, hung up before I stuck my foot in my mouth, and made a note to track down Leon for a date. Okay, so who wanted a full contingent in one place besides me? It meant somebody was still looking for Betty's fortune and thought that with enough publicity, some unsuspecting Joe would step forward and hand it over, or reveal that they'd been holding all Betty's assets in their cookie jar for donkey's years. Or they wouldn't step forward, but they wouldn't be able to resist showing up; and then they'd look guilty as hell and give themselves away. Prescott and Waite were the instigators. But Prescott didn't have to be Betty's murderer to be interested in acquiring the fortune she'd left to her daughter, a fortune that was legally his wife's to claim. And probably there'd be a payoff for Waite as legal executor — a percentage of Betty's millions? Would Kirkendahl show up? Would McGann? After all, I sighed, this event could be intended to distract us all from what was really going on. Maybe it was the result of an overflowing of generous impulses on the part of some good-hearted citizens. And maybe my housemates don't have hairballs.

But the memorial service was still over a week away. What was I going to do in the meantime, besides chalk up another goddamn period? I could start shooting lessons so I could show up at the event prepared, but it would be too frustrating to just hang out and do nothing.

I decided to practice another technique important to the professional detective: the stakeout.

The next morning, I donned dark glasses and plain clothes — khaki shorts and white T-shirt — and drove the beige bomber downtown in the tropical heat. I was going to park across from Waite's office building, but that was a 7–9 lane and it was only 8:50. So I drove around the block ten times, then settled into a parking space so that I was facing Waite's door. I dropped in my first two quarters. In the next hour, I polished off a package of sugar donuts and a Diet Coke. I checked the rearview mirror for sneak attackers twenty times. I sang every Motown song I could remember. I double-checked that the gun was in my glove compartment. I filed my nails. I soaked the seat with sweat. I wrote mental letters to my niece and two friends.

I'd gotten out to feed the meter at eleven when I spotted Waite coming up the sidewalk on the opposite side of the street. I ducked behind the car and wished I had a periscope. I peered at him over the hood. He didn't look villainous or murderous or nervous; he was just a man walking to the office. Bankers' hours were nothing to attorneys' hours. He went into the building. I slunk into the car. That was the end of the day's excitement.

By twelve o'clock I was going stir crazy. Plus I had to pee. And I wished I hadn't eaten all the donuts. I walked up the block to a little sandwich shop, ordered a cheeseburger to go, and went to the john. I would spend the rest of the day wondering if I'd missed something. The temperature inside the car rose, so I took to getting out and going for little strolls, wondering all the time which direction Waite's windows faced. Once I returned to find my meter had expired and damn near panicked. All I needed was to get in trouble with the law while transporting an unregistered handgun in the glove compartment.

Along about four o'clock, the cars parked around me started to clear out, and I realized that I was in a 4–6 lane as well. I decided I'd had enough for my first day out, especially since I couldn't be sure Waite was in the building anymore due to my two ten-minute bathroom breaks. I went home, settled into a cold bath with Spenser to see how he did it.

The next day I took a novel and a crossword puzzle book. Unprofessional, maybe, but I planned to discipline myself to look up every three minutes. I couldn't settle the bathroom question satisfactorily since I refused to take a can to piss in. If someone caught me at it, I'd be arrested for sure. Waite showed up at a quarter to eleven and disappeared inside. People came and went, but I didn't see a soul I recognized.

This was getting to be old hat. I wondered when the team of thugs would show up and threaten me, the way they always do Spenser. Two goddamn days, and as far as I could tell, nobody had noticed me except for the owner of the tattoo parlor next to my parking space, who took to waving at me. Even worse, I hadn't lost a pound despite all the sweating I'd done. Must have been the sugar donuts, cheeseburgers, ice cream bars, and potato chips. Time for isometrics: I tried holding my stomach in to a count of ten.

Don't ask me why I hung around after four that day. I guess I just wanted to see if Waite ever emerged from that fucking building. I found an unattended lot up the street, ignored the dire warnings about towing, got out and sat on the hood of the car, straining to see the front of the building. At five-thirty, Waite emerged. I started the car as he disappeared into a nearby parking garage. Now all I had to do was watch the two exits at once. I caught a glimpse of him in a white Caddy, but only because the tinted window hadn't slid up all the way yet. I pulled out.

He turned up Vine Street, then left on Garfield Place across from the public library. He eased up to the curb in front of the Cincinnati Club. I rounded the center island and for a wonder found a place to park on the opposite side, facing the club building.

The crowd seemed kind of heavy even for a Friday night at the Cincinnati Club. A whole string of BMWs, Caddies, and Lincoln Continentals rolled past the door. I wondered what was going on and why I hadn't been invited. Probably nobody from my neighborhood was there.

I nearly swallowed my teeth when I caught a glimpse of Kirkendahl headed up the sidewalk. I recognized him from my personal collection of mug shots. I got out of the car and started wondering how to get into that damn building. I crossed the street and was casing the joint when I ran into Fred's old boss from Procter and Gamble. He shook my hand, running an eye up and down appraisingly, and asked how I was doing in that tone people use with recent widows. I said that I was doing fine, and how was he doing, and what was he doing here. He said that somebody — don't ask me who, but some Republican — was announcing for City Council tonight, and he was attending the fundraising dinner. We parted with mutually insincere promises to keep in touch.

I found a phone on the corner and called Mel. I told her to go find Leon Jakes, get him into his best suit, and meet me back at my apartment. Then I headed home, taking the parkway to avoid traffic tie-ups on the freeway and watching out for cops.

At home, I dug out a nice grandmotherly polyester number and a pair of pantyhose (God, the sacrifices I make to duty!). I smeared on some makeup and found some lipstick I hadn't worn for a year. It crumbled a little, but once the heat hit it, it stuck. I pulled a purse down from the shelf, then realized that it wouldn't hold the revolver and traded it for a medium-sized bag. If the bag was too big, I reasoned, it would take me five minutes to find the gun, the way it does the car keys, and I'd probably blow a hole in the bottom of the purse looking for the damn thing.

Then I sat down and fidgeted. According to my watch, I'd called Mel forty-five minutes ago. *God send me a cash bar,* I pleaded. The minutes dragged on. Where could they be? Buying Leon a suit? My makeup was starting to run and the cats ignored me as if I were a Jehovah's Witness who happened to be camped in their living room.

The front door slammed and I made the hall in one step.

Leon looked magnificent: navy blazer, pale-blue shirt, dark blue paisley tie.

"It took Leon a while to decide what to wear," Mel explained.

"This my best Sunday suit. It okay, miss?"

"It's terrific, Leon. You'll be the handsomest guy there. Does your mother know where you are?"

"Uh-huh. M-mel ax her could I go out with another white lady for a while, and she say 'yes.'" I raised an eyebrow at Mel.

"Brevity is the soul of wit," she said. I pushed him out the door.

On the way downtown I explained to him. "Now, we're looking for the man you saw that Saturday with the old lady who got off the bus, remember?" He nodded. "We think maybe he killed that lady, which makes him a criminal. Now, the place we're going is holding a big dinner for important people, and I want you to look at two of those people and tell me whether either one of them is the man you saw when his baseball cap fell off. I want you to tell me the truth, now; don't just say it is because you want to make me happy. If you don't recognize either of these guys as the man you saw that day, I want you to tell me, understand?"

He nodded again. "Uh-huh."

Naturally, there wasn't a parking place in sight, so we had to park and walk damn near four blocks. Four blocks in pantyhose and high heels. I'm getting too old for this.

We lucked out. There was a camera crew from Channel 5 headed into the Cincinnati Club, and the cameraman was one of Sidney's fans from Tuesday night. He recognized me, and I asked if we could sort of tag along. I told him we were looking for somebody. He gave me a wink and we fell in.

We entered the back of a big banquet room. It was laid out in circular tables with a speaker's platform up front, presumably lined with dignitaries. The cameraman stopped to consider the layout, then headed up the side. We followed. I scanned the crowd for the faces I wanted Leon to see.

The cameraman had obviously timed his entrance to coincide with the beginning of the program. Knives and forks were still rattling when the first speaker got up and told folks to keep eating while the program commenced. Behind us, a waitress brought a tray full of sherbet and set it down to melt.

When I found Waite he was sitting only about five yards away. The man sitting next to him was Kirkendahl.

What happened next takes more time to tell than it did to happen. I nudged Leon and nodded at the table just as the cameraman turned his light onto the speaker's platform. As Leon craned his neck to see, some people turned around, their attention drawn to the cameraman by the light. Across the table from Harry Waite and Edgar P. Kirkendahl was Dr. Harrison Prescott. As he turned around, Leon shouted, "That's him!" In his excitement, he waved an arm, lost his balance, and fell backward into the tray of sherbet. In a sea of startled faces, I saw three. I reached up and grabbed hold of the cameraman's wrist and part of the light, which promptly burned the shit out of my hands. I swung the light around toward the audience and received a gratifying chorus of shouts and groans for my effort. I pulled a struggling Leon to his feet and dragged him to the exit. We beat a hasty retreat through the lobby, leaving a sticky rainbow trail behind us, with as much dignity as we could muster.

I had decided, after all, not to put the gun in my purse in case I was arrested for crashing the Cincinnati Club. Now I hoped we wouldn't get gunned down in the four blocks between here and the car. As I say, it wouldn't have been hard to track us.

"It was him! It was him!" Leon shouted as we rounded the corner.

I motioned for him to keep his voice down. "Which one was him?"

"The m-m-man. The man at the t-table. It was him." Ah, bittersweet victory.

"Which man?"

"The one at the table."

"Which one at the table? Was he facing you?"

"Yes."

"Did he have to turn around to face you?"

He considered. "I j-just saw his f-face. It was a white man, like I tole you. A tall white man, shorter than me."

"Can you say what he looked like?"

"Nuh-uh, but he was a white man, look like a judge or something. Dressed up."

He looked like a judge? What did a judge look like?

This conversation proceeded in much the same manner all the way home, so I won't bore you with the details. The upshot was that one of the men at the table was the man Leon saw with Betty on the day she was murdered. I just didn't know which one.

I tried to look on the bright side. Yesterday, I had ten suspects or more. Today I had three. Not bad for a beginner.

I pulled up outside Leon's house on Boyd Street and surveyed the damage. Why was I worried about being gunned down by a hardened killer? One look at Leon and his mother would kill me.

Just as long as nobody went after Leon.

CHAPTER 22

Mrs. Jakes, who was watering the yard when we pulled up, proved to be a philosophical woman with a sense of humor honed on raising seven children.

"Don't tell me what happened. I don't want to know. That child don't find dirt, it finds him."

He was her baby, but she had no illusions about him.

"It ain't a one of my seven could ever get as dirty as Leon could. He holds the family record in that department."

"I'm paying him for his time tonight, Mrs. Jakes, of course, and I'd like to give you something extra for the dry cleaners."

"Uh-uh, no, ma'am. No call for that. If it hadn't been tonight with you, it would've been some other way. We got an account down to Chase's Dry Cleaning. They send me the bill once a month. But if he done some work for you, why, you just pay him whatever you think is fair. Leon works for lots of folks, and I keep him in work clothes."

I fished in my purse and brought out a ten-dollar bill for Leon. I wasn't sure what the going rate was, being a novice, but he seemed impressed when I handed it to him.

"What that for?"

"That's for being my operative tonight. You know what an operative is?"

"Nuh-uh."

"You ever watch those detective shows on television? You know the guys that ride around with the detective sometimes, and help them out on a case, and rescue them when they need it? That's what you did tonight."

He beamed. "I did? What you call that — what I did?"

"You were my operative."

"A operative." He rolled it around on his tongue, and liked the sound of it. "A operative! Wait'll I t-tell Raymond and Charles! A operative!"

"Yeah, they be mighty impressed. 'Specially when they get a look at them pink and green stains you acquired in the line of duty. Now go on in the house and change." His mother shooed him off, making sure first that he thanked me for the money.

Now that I had a chance to talk to Mrs. Jakes in private, I wanted to warn her without frightening her out of her wits. Telling her that her baby boy was a witness to a murder boded fair to net me the wrong result. Still, I figured she had to know.

"Uh — how much did Mel tell you about the job Leon was doing for me, Mrs. Jakes?"

"Just that he was some kind of witness to a crime, and y'all was looking for the criminal."

"Yeah, well, it was a pretty big crime, I'm afraid. He saw somebody with a murder victim right before she was murdered."

"Not that old bag lady was killed a while back over across Hamilton?"

"That's the one."

"And it was another lady killed, too, just after that, downtown. A Black lady was a friend of the white lady."

"That's right."

"Uh, uh, uh." She shook her head. "What kind of folks is that, to go around murdering helpless old ladies ain't even got a roof over they head? That's some kind of meanness. And you say Leon maybe saw the murderer?"

"I think so. And he tried to identify the man tonight, but unfortunately, I didn't see which man he was pointing at. And I don't know whether the man he identified saw him."

"So we could be in trouble is what you telling me?"

"Well, yes. I guess I'm telling you to be cautious, is all."

"Do the police know about Leon?"

"Not yet, but I'll call them tonight so they can help keep an eye on him."

"Honey, I appreciate that, but the police gone say they got better things to do than watch my boy. I better let his brothers know about this."

"That's a good idea. Meanwhile, I plan to keep an eye on him myself."

"You got a gun?" I liked the way she said this. Not incredulously, as some would. She was just asking for the information.

"Yes, ma'am. And if somebody comes after Leon, I'll use it," I said, with more bravado than I felt.

I went home to change and to report in to Al and Mel. Kevin was at work, basking in the reflected glory of his famous feline neighbor.

"After tonight, I feel like I'd better keep an eye on Leon for a few days. If anything happened to him I'd hate myself. What if the killer — whoever he is — has known about Leon all the time and has just been waiting to see if he was going to talk?"

"I'll trade off with you, Cat, if you want," Mel volunteered. "I mean, I kind of feel invested in Leon's future too, now."

I accepted the offer gratefully and went downstairs to change while Al made me some coffee to take on my vigil. To tell the truth, after two days on a stakeout I was afraid I was going to get bedsores or hemorrhoids or something from sitting on my ass all that time. I put on jeans and a dark T-shirt along with my Adidas. I double-checked the revolver to make sure it was loaded the way Kevin had instructed me.

It occurred to me that Mel was better armed with her bare hands than I was with a goddamn handgun.

I called the station and asked for Fricke. Needless to say, he wasn't there. Probably home playing Parcheesi or watching "Starsky and Hutch" reruns. I called Landau at home and got a fucking answering machine. I had to call back to leave my message, I was so flustered; so much to tell, so little time before the beep.

I don't know if you've ever sat all night in a car in the dark in a quiet neighborhood before, but it's no fun. I brought my tape deck and earphones, drank coffee, ate a whole bag of Oreos, and peed behind the neighbors' rhododendrons. I saw one cruiser all night, and I ducked as it went past. So much for the watchful eye of the law.

I had lots of time to think that night, and I thought I knew who the murderer was. My reasons involved a lot of little clues, though, and this candidate could hardly be arrested on that basis. In fact, without Leon, it was hard to imagine him being arrested on any basis, so successfully had he covered his tracks so far.

I had a ringside seat at the kitty parade that passes every night between 1 a.m. and dawn. Big cats, small cats, cats with collars, cats without, mangy cats, rangy cats, toms and queens, cats with fleas and cats without. You couldn't tell their colors in the dark, but sometimes you could see their eyes. They were all on the prowl, moving sinuously and purposefully down the street, up the sidewalks, across the yards. At 3 a.m. there was a hell of a cat fight about half a block down, and I saw kitties watching from windows, but I resisted my maternal impulse and remained uninvolved. For all I knew, the killer could have hired two cats for the night to distract me, the way Sherlock Holmes always did it.

I had yawned so much my jaw ached when Mel turned up to relieve me at seven, bright-eyed and bushy-tailed, the way those healthy types always are. I reported no action, drove home, and crawled into bed.

When I woke up at one, Kevin was up and gone, leaving me a note to say that he'd relieve Mel until five. I called the station again, and this time got Fricke.

"What the hell are you up to now, Caliban? Landau gave me some kind of story about a witness that needed protection. If this is another one of your goddamned fairy tales, forget it."

On less than six hours of sleep, I have a short fuse.

"I haven't given you a goddamned thing that isn't useful information — information that you bozos should have had within a week of the Grumbacher murder. Now your only chance at bringing this case to prosecution is endangered, and you couldn't give a shit."

"What the hell are you talking about?"

"I'm talking about Leon Jakes. Have you interviewed Leon?"

"Who the hell is Leon Jakes?"

"He's a witness who can identify a man he saw Betty Grumbacher with just before she was killed. Why do I have to tell you this?"

"Well, who the hell is endangering this Jakes guy?" I noticed he neither contradicted me nor softened his tone. He was going to tough it out.

"I took Leon to a dinner last night and pointed out a table where three men were sitting — three men connected to the case. Leon identified one of them."

"Oh, yeah? Are you going to tell me who, or are we playing twenty questions?"

"I can't tell you who, because Leon isn't very articulate, and I couldn't tell who he was pointing at." I matched his tone. If he could ignore his mistakes, I could ignore mine.

"How old is this Leon?" Fricke demanded suspiciously.

"Old enough. Christ, I'm telling you the murderer is one of three men; do I have to do everything for you?"

"Were there only three men at the fucking table?"

"No," I admitted.

"Then how the hell do you know it was one of those three?"

"Because they're the only three guys at the table with motives and connections to Grumbacher." I wasn't absolutely sure about this and he didn't buy it.

"As far as you know. Look, tell me who you're talking about, and I'll check into it. Then I'll follow up on this Leon Jakes character. Will that make you happy?"

He'd switched again to patronizing me. I liked him better belligerent. He snorted at my three names and I wondered if he was really writing them down. Hell, Waite and Kirkendahl probably had the entire police force in their pockets. He took down Leon's name and address.

"Anything else, Mrs. Caliban?" he said.

"Yeah. Don't sit around with your thumb up your ass on this one, Sarge. The last time you did that, another person wound up dead. If anything happens to Leon—"

He hung up on me.

* * *

For nearly four days, I trailed Leon. Or rather, we trailed Leon. Every now and then, some new player would turn up, someone I didn't recognize, and whisper hoarsely, "O'Neill sent me." Then we'd run through a litany of questions so I'd know the guy (and it was always a guy) was genuine. Who's Kevin's favorite female vocalist? What's the special ingredient in his salad dressing? What color is the stain on the back of his Boston Celtics T-shirt? Stuff like that. Kevin's recruits all looked like they could crush a criminal to the thickness of a manhole cover just by leaning on him. They were a reassuring bunch. All the same, by the third day of sleep deprivation, I was getting too goddamned foggy to remember the answers to my own questions, and I began to consider ordering team shirts from La Pooch.

On Monday Kevin called me at four to tell me that Leon was working at Len's Lounge, so I met Kevin out front at four thirty. He'd been inside drinking beer, since he'd only seen poor photographs of the suspects, and he didn't want to stay outside in case he missed them coming in. The beer was cold, he said, and the company was congenial. But I wanted to keep a clear head.

Len's was popular with the after-work crowd, so at least I had more to look at than I'd had all day Sunday, when the high point of my day was the after-church lunch stakeout at the Blue Jay diner. I was cruising the window of the junk shop next door for about the fiftieth time when I caught sight of a man ambling up the sidewalk. He was dressed in jeans and a T-shirt and a jacket — a goddamn jacket in August. He was wearing one of those goofy-looking sailor hats with the rim pulled down, the way they wear them on the back nine. I supposed he was checking out the neighborhood from behind his Foster Grants, but I couldn't tell.

He pushed open the door of Len's Lounge and went in. He looked as suspicious as a military haircut at a socialist convention. I glanced around for a cruiser, but they were all busy clearing out the 4–6 lanes. No luck. I counted to ten and went in. The place was dim, and it took me a minute to adjust my eyes. The guy in the goofy hat was disappearing through a door in the back. The son of a bitch was counting on his disguise, the dim lighting, and the distraction of the television to guard his anonymity. I didn't think he'd come in to use the john. I had the gun shoved into my waistband, with a loose-fitting shirt covering it. I was sure Kevin wouldn't approve of the way I was carrying it, but I didn't have time to obtain the O'Neill Seal. I nodded at the boys at the bar as I reached for it. I think they thought I was a pregnant woman experiencing labor pains. Well, maybe not. I listened at the door, but the goddamn television was turned up so loud I couldn't hear anything. I pushed through the door with the gun drawn. I was in the kitchen. The back door was open and through it I could see daylight. I knew from previous reconnoitering that behind the building was a fairly large parking lot — the kind you might use if you weren't too fond of your hubcaps and were shopping for an easy insurance loss.

I peeked around the side of the door. He was walking across the lot with his arm around Leon, headed toward another building with a high fence around the yard. I figured he was trying to get away from the bar crowd, and I couldn't see if he was holding a gun on Leon.

I wasn't even sure of my range, but I doubted my ability to follow him surreptitiously on my little Cat feet. My eye snagged a half-empty beer bottle at my feet, and I tried the oldest trick in the book. I heaved it at the side of a rusty pick-up parked some fifteen feet away from me. It shattered with a satisfying crash, and he wheeled around. Being old counts for something.

For a second I was afraid he was going to take out the pick-up and my fucking insurance company would reclassify me as an uninsurable risk in my new line of work.

I gave the door a little shove and said, in my deepest, most menacing voice, "Drop it!"

He turned his head and stared at me. Or I guess he was staring at me; with the shades it was hard to tell. Leon was standing patiently by, minding his own business, just waiting for the seasons to change.

"Go ahead. Make my day." It was the first goddamn thing that came into my head, I'm ashamed to admit. I needed better role models.

He moved. As he did, I flinched, and the back door struck the wall and bounced back. There was an explosion and the sound of splintering wood. As the door swung back, I pointed the gun at him and squeezed the trigger. Nothing happened. *Damn it to bloody hell,* I thought, *who is it always tells her youngest daughter you get what you pay for?* Lost and found my eye. Freebie firearms. Then all at once there was this terrific crack and I felt my arms jerk, just about the time Leon fell backward over a line of garbage cans and sent one crashing into his assailant's shins. I hadn't seen the garbage cans before. I honest-to-God think they materialized just so Leon could trip over them. I didn't know immediately which of us had gotten the guy, but one of us had. He went over backward and his gun went flying. Ditto the goofy hat.

"The gun, Leon! Pick up the gun!"

The guy made a grab for it, and Leon stepped on his hand in the excitement. Even then, I don't think Leon was deliberately trying to hurt the bastard. Leon came up with the gun and I told him to hold it very carefully flat in the palm of his hand. People from the bar were beginning to crowd around and I didn't want Leon to trip again and wipe them all out. I held my gun on the battered figure on the ground and tried to ignore the shooting pains in my elbow where I'd whacked it against the door.

"Dr. Prescott, I'm making a citizen's arrest. I'm arresting you for the murders of Betty Grumbacher, your mother-in-law, and Lucille Thornbush Shelton." That's how they do it on the "Andy Griffith Show," sort of.

"Leon," I said. "You're a goddamn hero."

CHAPTER 23

"But you knew it would be Prescott," Al said as we sat around the living room the next day celebrating with Graeter's black raspberry chip ice cream. Kevin was eating it for breakfast, only slightly mollified for having missed the climactic shoot-out at Len's. "How come?" We lay in various stages of gluttonous collapse and the three kitties had their heads buried in the bowls.

"I wouldn't say I *knew* it," I corrected. "I suspected it. First off, the Prescotts are the ones who legally inherited the Grumbacher fortune, assuming there was one, so if Betty still had the Velazquez emerald, it now belonged to them. When the Prescotts became involved in organizing the memorial service, I figured the good doctor expected to profit from Betty's death. And also that he hadn't yet figured out where to look for Betty's assets."

"But Mrs. Prescott said the service might have been Waite's idea," Al persisted.

"That's true, and I knew all along that if Prescott were in it, he had to be relying on information from Waite. It was possible that Waite had organized the service to shake loose some information he could use himself, but how likely was that? When people come to a memorial service, they don't seek out the family attorney if they have a story to tell — they go to the family.

"Anyway, I had gone back to one of my original questions: who did Betty trust enough to follow here? And why? Waite was a possibility; she'd known him for a long time. So were McGann and her pals from the soup kitchen. But Kirkendahl? All of her friends said Betty was a suspicious woman. I don't think she would have followed Kirkendahl through an emergency exit in a four-alarm fire. Grunewald she had no reason to suspect of wishing her harm, but she wouldn't have diverged from her accustomed path on his account. In fact, when you think about it, Betty's Saturday cemetery visit was such established routine that it would take something pretty important to interrupt that. I could think of several scenarios, but the one I kept returning to involved the daughter she'd lost so tragically — the daughter she was saving her fortune for, the daughter she had secretly watched for years. Maybe she'd seen Prescott before, or maybe he was able to convince her to go with him because he made his story plausible enough."

"What do you think he told her?" Mel asked.

"I don't know. I imagine he told her about some emergency — her daughter had been involved in an accident, or knew about her and wanted to see her. It could have been anything, as long as she didn't expect to be taken out to Montgomery, where the Prescotts lived."

"But how did he get into the apartment — Prescott, I mean?" Kevin wanted to know.

"I don't know that yet. But I have an idea. Remember your old pal, Connie Steinfirst? The one who went to California to heal her broken heart in a hot tub?"

"You don't think Connie was having an affair with Dr. Prescott? It gives me the creeps just to think such a thing!"

"No, but what if she were having an affair with good-time Harry Waite? As a receptionist for one law firm, she would be likely to meet lawyers from other firms, and his tastes definitely run to sweet young things. Of course, this is pure speculation."

"Then Harry might have a key. But didn't that suggest that Harry was the murderer?"

"It could. But I still thought it was someone with a legitimate claim to Betty's fortune. Otherwise, why kill her? My problem was not recognizing how many opportunities rich professional men like Waite and Prescott have to meet each other. I'm such a fucking dolt, I checked the Cincinnati Club and Queen City Club membership lists, but the goddamn country club didn't occur to me."

"You move in the wrong circles, Mrs. C," Kevin commiserated. "You couldn't be expected to think like a wealthy bastard of a gynecologist."

"Yeah, but I even knew they both played golf. Prescott came in from the links the day I first met him and Waite talked about his goddamn golf game. You'd think I was waiting for the fucking duck to descend."

"But I still don't see why Prescott killed Betty," Al said. "He didn't know where her money was."

"No, but he's such an arrogant son of a bitch, I bet he thought he could figure it out. Maybe he asked her where it was, and she got suspicious."

"Hell, don't you think she was suspicious when he brought her to an empty apartment?"

"Maybe that's what did it. I assume she pulled the knife on him at some point in the conversation, rightly perceiving that she was in danger. He disarmed her, maybe held a gun on her, then killed her with her own knife, either in the heat of the moment or because he thought he'd ruined his chances with her. As a doctor, he didn't have any trouble figuring out where to aim. Then he searched her and took her shopping bags, assuming he'd find something in them to tell him where to look. After all, he could 'find' Betty's fortune surreptitiously or publicly — it didn't matter, since his wife was her legal heir."

"But she foxed him," Kevin enthused.

"Yep, she sure did. He didn't find anything. So he went after Lucille, who guarded Betty's secret with her life."

"Yeah, but why did Prescott suddenly decide to push the issue when all's he had to do was wait for Betty to die and he'd inherit?" Mel asked.

"His old golfing pal Harry Waite — the same pal who'd told him he stood to inherit the Grumbacher fortune to begin with — tipped him off that the old girl was starting to spend her money foolishly — giving contributions to organizations for the homeless. She might give away a substantial amount of the fortune Prescott had his eye on, or even — perish the thought — change her will. Waite would make a few measly hundred off the will revision, but he was looking for bigger game: the legal fees involved in handling a large estate can buy a hell of a lot of golf balls. Plus, he probably expected a kickback from Prescott if Prescott inherited."

"Blackmail?" Al asked.

"Maybe, especially if he gave Prescott the key. Who knows?"

"Yeah, but how is Helen Prescott involved? Did she know all this was going on?"

"My guess is no, but her husband and his attorney are running a pretty tight ship and we may never know what she really thinks or feels."

"Do you think he'll plea bargain?"

"Are you kidding? An arrogant son of a bitch like that? As far as the two murders are concerned, all the evidence is circumstantial. When they searched Prescott's office, they found objects the St. Francis crowd have identified as the contents of Betty's and Lucille's shopping bags. But not, for example, Lucille's clothing, or anything with Betty's blood on it. And when the shopping bag stuff is introduced in court, he can say either that he never saw it before, or that it was stuff he'd had for years and the street people are crazy. He might actually get indicted for the attack on Leon since there are witnesses, but his story is that Leon attacked *him*, and he pulled a gun in self-defense. As for Leon's identification of him, it'll be his word against Leon's. Whether or not the jury will believe a mentally handicapped kid instead of an eminent physician is up for grabs."

"Speaking of guns," said Kevin, "whatever happened to that little .38 Special I gave you?"

"Beats me. The cops found a gun in a garbage can when they searched the parking lot, but it didn't have any fingerprints on it and it wasn't registered to anybody. By that time, a large percentage of Len's clientele was camped on Prescott's chest. Could that be the .38 you lost?"

"Now, Mrs. C," he grumbled, "I don't want you to go getting the idea that I can pull firearms out of a hat or anything. I wish you'd take better care of the things I give you."

"Okay, say the jury accepts Leon's story and Prescott is convicted." Mel was pursuing her own line of thought. "He can't profit from his crime, right, Al?"

"No, but his wife can, I think, as long as she's not an accessory."

"Yeah, but we still don't know whether there is any profit," Kevin burst out. "You said Lucille died to guard Betty's secret, but what secret is that? She swallowed the key to a safe deposit box, okay, but the emeralds weren't there, as I recall."

"That's the real stumper," I said ruefully. "I looked at those goddamn articles again this morning. I know there must be something in them, but what? Every new brainstorm I get is more wacko than the last."

"Yeah, but the most wacko thing of all would be if it turned out Betty didn't have a dime to her name after all and she and Lucille died for nothing."

CHAPTER 24

I don't go to church any more than I have to. I don't have anything against organized religion; I just don't want to be part of the organization. Churches always make me feel either guilty or giddy. As for religious ceremonies, like weddings and funerals, they both require a leap of faith I just can't make. If I ever meet Saint Peter, he'll have to weigh my faults against my honesty. But I wouldn't have missed Betty's memorial service for this world and the other one combined. I had a feeling it would be quite an affair.

I was right. Imagine, if you will, a cross between the Academy Awards ceremony and a Southern Baptist revival meeting, and you will have something of the flavor of it. I'll say that for Helen Prescott: once she made sure that Lucille was included, she went all the way.

We all four put on our best clothes and went. I parked the beige bomber between a Coup de Ville and a rusty Studebaker. Even that didn't begin to describe the range, though. Some guests had hoofed it, while the stretch limos had been sent out to drive around during the service because there was no place to park them.

The outfits were something else again, and you couldn't tell by looking who was a movie star and who came from

Over-the-Rhine. Obviously, folks from the neighborhood weren't about to be outdone by the folks from Hollywood. The first couple that caught my eye turned out to be Curtis, in a smashing charcoal-gray three-piece suit that he'd either borrowed or salvaged and kept hidden over the years, and Trish, whose fairy godmother must have given Goodwill a little help. Even Jinks appeared to have shaved and turned up a clean white shirt for the occasion.

There was a troubling odor of mothballs that blended with the smell of flowers in the church. Some of the people looked as if they'd emerged from mothballs themselves. An energetic petite woman pushed past us up the aisle and Kevin grabbed my elbow. "*Lillian Gish!*" he breathed, in a stage whisper.

It nearly turned my stomach to see Prescott and Waite up front, although I'd expected it. Prescott had a good attorney, after all, and could afford the kind of bail set for respectable citizens accused of murdering undesirables. Helen Prescott looked very pale. Even from where we stood I could see how drained she looked, eyes sunken as if she hadn't been getting much sleep. Then, from behind me, I heard a familiar deep, raspy voice, louder than the respectful whispers buzzing around me.

"What the bloody hell is the goddamn *murderer* doing at a goddamn *memorial* service for the women he murdered? Don't those flaming assholes at the goddamn SAG know *anything* about propriety? Jesus Christ, if that was *my* union, I'd resign this fucking instant!"

It was the fastest mouth on both coasts: P. C. Stinger.

She was shorter than me, slightly built, but she looked taller, if you know what I mean. She had presence. She was dressed in some kind of pants outfit made out of yards and yards of flowing black material. She had gray hair, cut short like mine, and black eyes that could have skewered Harrison Prescott to the cross that hung suspended over the altar. She was releasing a stream of cigarette smoke along with the invective.

"Goddamn *sacrilege* is what it is." She stopped abruptly and looked at me.

"Cat Caliban, Phyl," I said, and stuck out my hand.

"Well, thank God," she said, shaking it with a grip I hope to emulate at ninety. "I was beginning to think I was alone amid the goddamn murderers and thieves."

We edged over and made room for her. Kevin was enthralled.

"Lilly looks good, doesn't she? It's those sweet-faced women who hold up, not the bitchy types like me and Betty," she cackled.

"You look okay to me," I said. Kevin was incapable of saying anything.

"I look alive, sweetie; that's what counts. I look alive."

I nodded toward the front of the church. "Aren't you speaking?"

She shook her head. "I think somebody informed them that this mouth is registered as a lethal weapon in four states and two foreign countries. They had, shall we say, second thoughts."

Too bad, I thought. Grunewald will put me to sleep, and I need to stay on my mettle.

Don't ask me who spoke. Between Kevin's gasps on one side and Phyl's running commentary on the other, I gathered that some of them were famous, but Gish was the only one I recognized. Grunewald did a half-decent job, for a goddamn pedant. I could've done without the "morning star" motif that kept popping up in his speech, but he wasn't as bad as I expected him to be.

Then a Black man, Dr. Somebody-or-Other from UCLA, stood up to speak about Lucille. He started out quietly, but what he said was so worth hearing you could hear the damn lilies shedding petals in the background. He talked matter-of-factly about Lucille's family, her parents working days at the slaughterhouses, her father putting in nights at local theaters and clubs after marriage induced him to retire from a musical comedy troupe. Lucille had grown up around theater, had read Shakespeare along with the Bible, and had once played Topsy in a rare mixed-race production of *Uncle Tom's Cabin.* A white girl named Betty Grumbacher had played Little Eva. The show had closed after five performances because of KKK threats to burn down the hall where it was playing, and the friendship between the two girls had run up against the geographical and social barriers erected by racism.

When Lucille had tried her luck in Hollywood at last, she had known the cards were stacked against her. With her father's support, whatever happened, she was determined to try. But jobs were hard to come by. After her first film, in which she played a maid to a wealthy socialite, the leading lady had offered Lucille a job as her personal maid. Lucille accepted; a job was a job. Altogether, she had remained in California for five years. Many of her acting jobs were acquired through the good graces of her old friend Betty Grumbacher, now Leda Marrs, whose maid she'd played in *Dangerous Lady*, and who claimed to be less interested in and less skilled at acting than Lucille. Lucille's favorite jobs were for the white-owned Black production companies, but these came along too infrequently. At last, she had given up and gone home to Cincinnati to work at the slaughterhouse like her mother and father. In 1929 she had married, but then her husband had developed the medical problem Sophronia Hewlett had mentioned and became disabled. He'd died of cancer in the forties.

Lucille had tried to join the service in 1943, but the medical examination had revealed a congenital heart defect. She was rejected and advised to avoid strenuous labor — the only kind of labor available to Black women. She trained to be a nurse and went to work for the Visiting Nurses Association. In 1948, she contracted a particularly virulent strain of influenza. She never recovered, physically or financially. No one could say for sure when she joined the ranks of the homeless. Eventually, the only family she saw was her cousin Sophronia. She lived on the streets with her friend, Betty Grumbacher:

two old ladies, living by their wits on the leftovers of others. She had died terrified but determined to protect her friend's secrets.

By this point, people were sobbing openly, and I craned my neck to see if the weight of moral censure in the church would rise and crush Prescott where he sat. I only saw the back of his head, and it looked undamaged and unbowed.

The speaker concluded by saying that although Lucille had been a unique and precious individual, her story repeated the stories of so many Black actresses. He wanted us to pray for all of them as we prayed for Lucille, and he named some of them, including Cincinnati's own Louise Beavers, rolling out the names like subdued thunder. When he finished, I felt exhausted.

As the final speakers rose to pay tribute, I became aware of a sniffling to my right that didn't come from any of my party. I leaned forward and peered down the row. At the very end was an elderly man with a cane, white wispy hair and gold-rimmed glasses. He was weeping into his handkerchief, apparently so distracted by grief that he didn't make it to his feet for the final hymn. I excused myself to Phyl, and as soon as the service ended, I slid along the row, moving against the crowd, which had decided not to disturb the old man to make its exit.

I offered him a clean handkerchief. I had brought a big supply for this purpose.

"Did you know her well?" I asked in sympathetic tones, expecting to hear that he had been Betty's plumber or druggist. I noticed a Bible sitting precariously on his lap.

"Yes, I-I'm her husband."

Well, whatever I had hoped for at this service, I hadn't dared to hope for this, and when it came I sat there stunned.

"Mr. Wilcox?"

"No, my name is Smith. Walter Smith. You must think I'm terrible, sitting here like this, but I — that is, we'd been separated for many years, and—"

Eureka! I'd discovered the long-lost husband at last, or at least one of them. I *knew* Betty had been the marrying kind.

"Separated? You mean . . . ?"

"Oh, no." He looked at me gravely. "We never divorced. I didn't believe in it, and my church didn't recognize divorce."

I caught Kevin out of the comer of my eye and tried to give him a significant nod. As my gaze swept the crowd, I found myself wondering how many more there were like this fellow.

"She didn't mind about the divorce. She said she'd already been divorced." He gave me a perplexed look that said he hadn't understood that Betty had been making a joke.

"Well," he said, gripping his cane, "I don't want to bore you."

"Oh, you're not boring me at all," I hastened to assure him. "As a matter of fact, I'm hoping maybe you know something about Betty that can solve the remaining mysteries surrounding her death."

He shot me a frightened glance. "You ain't a newspaper reporter? Or the police?"

"Neither. I'm a private investigator and I've been looking into Betty's murder. I'd very much appreciate it if you have some time now, if we could go somewhere and talk."

"Well, I suppose if you're not a reporter—"

I saw Kevin in one corner, Mel in another. Al was nowhere in sight. They had their instructions. They were supposed to separate, mingle, and keep their ears and eyes open.

"Listen, why don't we walk up the street to Wendy's and get some coffee? I'd really like to talk."

He was a slow walker. At the corner he paused to contemplate a wheelchair ramp.

"I haven't been downtown in a long time," he said. "I used to know the city like the back of my hand, seeing as how I was working in the city engineer's office. But there's been a lot of changes since my day. Take these ramps here. Simple enough thing to do, and useful to all kinds of folks — not just people in wheelchairs, but elderly folk like me with canes and walkers and bad eyesight, and young mothers with baby carriages, and delivery people with carts. Wish I'd thought of it." He shook his head. "Never even crossed my mind."

I got him settled in a booth in Wendy's with a cup of coffee and asked him how he'd met Betty. His weak blue eyes looked kind of moist and unfocused, but I couldn't tell whether that was nostalgia or cataracts. He had a high, thin voice.

"It was back in '47. I was a widower then, and feeling kind of lonely. I lived out in Clermont County, but I worked in the city. You could do that then; they didn't encourage it, but there wasn't no regulations against it like there is now. Well, I joined this here Christian singles group in town, and that's where I met Betty."

Christian singles? *Betty?*

"She seemed like a nice, quiet, refined Christian lady, good company, you know. She lived with her mother, and somehow I got to thinking she was a widow lady. I can't recollect now why I thought that, but I did. Well, we got on together, so by and by I asked her to tie the knot. And she agreed. So, we had a little service at my home congregation in Clermont—"

Clermont County! I caught my fist on its way to pummeling my forehead. Shit, I'd lived in Cincinnati for thirty years. You'd think it would have occurred to me that there was more than one county in the Greater Cincinnati area. And you don't find Clermont County marriages registered in the Hamilton County Courthouse.

"—and we moved into a house in College Hill. Wasn't so many colored there then as there is now, you know." He told me this as if he needed to justify his residence there. I didn't tell him that I lived in the general vicinity, in a neighborhood he would have considered downright disreputable on too many scores to count. I figured he was too old to adjust his view of the world.

"Well, sir, I thought things was going fine. We joined a square dance group, and I joined the church choir."

I was straining to picture Betty in this phase of her life. I couldn't.

"It went on like that for eight months, just about. Then one day I come home from work and find her sitting in the living room in the dark, with the shades drawn and no supper in the oven. She had this wooden crate on the floor beside her. It looked like something that maybe come in the mail, I don't know. And she had something looked like a letter laying in her lap. And she—" Here he stumbled, fumbled for words. "She'd been drinking. There was a bottle of whiskey on the floor. I could smell it in the room. Well, I — I'd never seen her like that before, I couldn't believe my eyes. I'd never seen her take a drink in all the time I'd known her. Why, I don't believe we would have — I mean, I wouldn't have — why, I don't hold with the taking of strong spirits. I've never taken a drink in my life. Our Lord drank only wine, and what was good enough for him is good enough for me."

I didn't ask him how much wine he drank. I was afraid to throw him off the track. His hand shook as he raised his coffee cup.

"But I don't want you to think I held it against her. No, sir. I thought, well, she's had bad news today, something has happened. Because she was in a strange mood, like. It was more than the liquor. We started to talk. And she said, 'It's over, Walter. I can't go on like this. You're a good man, and I've tried to be a good wife, but it just won't work out this way. I'm sorry.'" He paused for a minute again, and a tear worked its way down his cheek and dropped on the table.

"Why, you could have knocked me over with a feather. I hadn't no clue that she was unhappy, never even imagined she was. I reckon I thought that I was happy, and she seemed always the same, and so I hadn't no idea. I tried to talk to her about it. I thought she was just upset over something, like I said. Over the time I'd known her, I'd begun to have a suspicion she'd had some kind of health problems before, but I didn't know what they was, and she'd seemed okay to me. I thought maybe she'd got bad news about her health.

"But it wasn't nothing like that, she said. She said I didn't really know her, didn't know anything about her past. She said she'd thought she could change but she couldn't. I don't know what I thought she meant — maybe that she had a criminal record or something, I don't know. But then it all come out — how she'd been a big movie star out in Hollywood, and had been married before, more than once, and how she'd lived in a big mansion and drank champagne for breakfast and — and had a child by a man she wasn't even married to. I hadn't *no idea*, you see. I don't go to the cinema much, unless it's a religious picture, and that wasn't the kind she'd made. I hadn't no idea."

My heart went out to the poor old man, still baffled after all these years about how he could have lived with a woman for so long and known so little about her. But I knew, from personal experience, how credible it all was. Still, my assessment of Betty's acting abilities had changed dramatically in the past ten minutes.

"Well, I was willing to help her change, shocked as I was by everything she told me. My feelings were hurt pretty bad, too, on account of the things she'd kept from me. But I was still willing. I *loved* Betty, don't you see, and I wanted to keep her. But she said no, it wouldn't work out. So we talked it over, peaceful-like, and agreed to separate. Like I said, she didn't ask me to go against my religion and get a divorce, so I always considered her my wife, even when I hadn't seen her or heard from her for years. When I retired, I moved back to Clermont County to be near my sister and brothers, so I didn't hardly ever come to town at all. But I had an address, and I sent her a card every Christmas, and most years, why, she sent one to me. So I hadn't no way of knowing—"

He hitched up in his seat and fished a handkerchief out of his pants pocket, and wiped his eyes.

"If I'da knowed she was in need, if she'd only told me, why, I would've helped her. Maybe you think I held a grudge against her, but I didn't. I knew she'd tried to make things work out with me, and after we'd talked that day, I could see how it had been for her, and how hard she'd tried. I would've given the shirt off my back to take care of that woman. And to think she'd been living on the streets all those years! And then to die in such a horrible way! Why, I couldn't understand it at all."

"If it makes you feel any better, I think she was happier living on the streets and feeling that she was independent than she would have been if you'd paid rent on a luxury apartment for her. I don't think she would have accepted your generosity. But there's something else, too. In her will, she left everything to her daughter."

"That dark-haired lady up in front of the church?"

"That's right. Mrs. Prescott. And many people seem to feel that she had something to leave, perhaps even a great deal to leave. Did you ever have the impression that she might be very wealthy?" This was a shot in the dark. Clearly, he hadn't known much at all about the woman he'd married.

"Betty? No, I never thought she was rich. I believe she had some bank accounts of her own, but I didn't ask about that. I never wanted to meddle in her affairs. If we'da been younger, maybe it would've been different. But when you marry like we did, you don't feel like you have a right to pry."

"Did you ever see an emerald necklace, or any other jewelry she owned?"

"An emerald necklace? No, I never seen nothing like that. She had some costume jewelry, that was all. I don't believe it was anything valuable."

"Did she have any secret hiding places that you knew of, where she might have kept any valuables she might have had?"

"No, I don't know of any. Of course, she still had a lot of stuff over at her mother's. She could've left something over there."

I considered this angle. It had potential.

"Do you know when that house was sold?"

"I don't know as I recollect. Seems like it was in the early sixties, some time in there."

"I can find out the address, but you wouldn't happen to know it offhand?"

"No, I don't remember. Only that it was over in Westwood, off Montana somewhere."

"Can you think of anything else that might be helpful?"

"No, can't say's I can. I don't believe Betty was rich, though. Why would she've lived on the streets if she was rich?"

"A lot of people are asking that question."

We exchanged phone numbers. I thanked him and told him to call me if he thought of anything, however small, that might be useful. I walked him to his car, an old blue Rambler.

I caught up with my group at a post-funeral reception at the Hilton. I collared Grunewald and asked if he remembered Mrs. Grumbacher's address in Westwood. He said she'd lived on Millrich; he couldn't remember the number but referred me to his book — a copy of which lay open on the reception table. It was 3418.

I ducked out and called Landau, who happened to be in place, for once. I asked whether it would be possible to search Betty's mother's house at 3418 Millrich on the suspicion that she had hidden valuable jewelry there. He said, "Hold on," and went away.

When he came back, he said, "It might be possible, but we'd have to be smarter than the last guys who did it. We had a B and E there three weeks ago, and the place was ransacked."

CHAPTER 25

I admit I wanted to take a crack at 3418 Millrich myself. Whoever had done the job before, I felt damn sure it hadn't been a mother. Which meant, to my mind, that they didn't have the proper experience — had never scoured a house for a missing tennis shoe, the necklace somebody's aunt had given a kid for their birthday, or a missing library book. But what were the chances that Fricke would let me within a mile of the place? So I did an end run around him. I got the name of the owners from Landau by pointing out that I could check the newspaper files for police reports, or go to the neighborhood and ask around, or whatever. So he told me their name was Stewart.

Meanwhile, the reception was winding down in the other room. Most of the movie stars had followed the press out. The Prescotts had left early, according to my informants, because they had no doubt noticed an isolation zone that followed them around. But the soup kitchen crowd was still flocked around the hors d'oeuvres table, and would be until the last empty platter retreated into the kitchen. Some of them dropped tidbits unabashedly into their shopping bags; others, more discreet, simply pocketed them or slipped them into handbags.

Kevin was having an animated conversation with Curtis and Trish, while Phyl Stinger, who appeared to be smashed, was holding court in the corner, encouraged by Obie. Jinks was snoring softly into a potted palm. It was half an hour before I rounded up my troops and headed out.

We sat around Kevin's kitchen table with the air conditioner making a comforting hum in the background. Everybody had pitched their dress uniforms and we were all in shorts. Kevin was making tomato sauce. I was taking notes.

"So somebody already searched this house, okay, but how do we know they didn't find anything?" Al was playing with Sophie's tail, which was hanging over the nearest windowsill.

"We don't. We might guess that because the reception was organized after the house was searched, Prescott and Waite hadn't found what they were looking for yet and were still hoping to find additional information."

"But we don't even know that they're the only ones looking, do we?"

"Nope."

"And why would Prescott risk getting caught searching the house — or hiring somebody to do it — if he was the legal heir?"

"Because it might be hard to convince the police and the Stewarts to allow some stranger to come in and ransack the place the way it was apparently ransacked."

"Do we think the person that broke into the Stewart house was the same guy that broke in here?" Mel asked. "What was his name? Richie somebody?"

"No, Landau says the job didn't have Richie's finesse, if you can think of that as a word applicable to a guy staggering around with a cat stuck to his head. I'm not sure I think the two were related. I don't think we can assume that. Anyway, I want to hear from you guys. Meet anybody interesting at church today?"

"I talked to a woman who knew both Betty and Lucille in California in their salad days," Kevin offered. "She said Lucille was a fine actress who never got a chance. She said Betty was wild, and probably drank up everything she earned."

"I talked to a woman who did occasional housekeeping for Betty and her mother over the years," Al said. We all looked at her. "No, she didn't think Betty had a lot of money, but she did describe something odd. She said there was a funny pile of old crates in the basement, lying on their sides. Said they took up half the basement."

"Walter Smith said Betty had received a crate in the mail the day their marriage broke up," I said excitedly. "It must have had some emotional significance for her, because when he got home from work that day, his sweet Christian ladylove was blotto."

"Yeah, well, I asked her what she thought they were, and she said she'd asked Betty that. She said Betty said, 'Those are the love of my life.' Then she'd laughed and said they were just a bunch of old crates — stuff they'd inherited from some relative who'd died."

"Half the basement, though." I groaned. "If there was still something around that took up half a basement, don't you think somebody would have found it by now?"

"Maybe she had an old Isotta Fraschini, like Gloria Swanson had in *Sunset Boulevard*, and somebody was shipping it to her in pieces. If it were put back together, it'd probably be worth a fortune," Kevin suggested.

"Yeah, but where are the pieces now?" Mel asked. "They could be spread all over the city for all we know."

Her words tugged at my brain, but they didn't loosen up anything except dandruff.

"I met a guy who knew a guy who knew Wilcox, one of Betty's exes," said Kevin. "I asked if Wilcox knew that Betty had died and he said he didn't think Wilcox knew whether Wilcox had died. So I guess your information there was accurate, Mrs. C."

"Anybody notice any Arab types?"

"Not one." Kevin sighed. "Believe me, I'd notice. Looks like you take the trick, Mrs. C. You came up with a husband to

Al's housekeeper, Mel's insurance agent, and my old acquaintance. Looks like you get the P.I. license."

"Yeah, I'll make sure I include that on my application form: 'Once found husband when he landed in same pew at memorial service.'"

"You only have to tell the truth on those forms, Cat," Al reminded me. "It doesn't say anything about the whole truth."

"So what's next?" Mel asked.

"I suppose I go visit the Stewarts," I said. "Unless I want to take out an ad in the newspaper: 'Wanted. Information leading to recovery of priceless emerald necklace owned by murdered bag lady.'"

"After tomorrow," Kevin said prophetically, "I'll bet you won't have to."

CHAPTER 26

He was right, as usual. The morning *Post* featured a big spread on the memorial service on the front page of the Metro section and a box story with the headline, "Police, Heirs Hunt for Missing Jewels of Leda Marrs." At the bottom was a close-up of the necklace, the first one I'd seen. Maybe the cops had dug up an old insurance photo and had given it to the press to run in the hope that the emerald would turn up.

So I dressed in a modest, respectable cotton skirt and blouse, took the paper with me, and went to see the Stewarts.

A kid answered the door.

"Hey, Ma, there's somebody here to see you! It's a lady!"

Cats you can train to answer the door. Kids and dogs, never.

Mr. Stewart came to the door, paper in hand.

"I hope I'm not disturbing you," I said, smiling what I hoped was a disarming smile.

"We're eating breakfast," he said noncommittally.

"I see you've been reading the *Post*. I brought it with me, because I'd hoped to interest you in one of the stories, which I believe has a connection with your recent break-in. My name is Catherine Caliban, and I've been investigating a case that I think is related. May I come in and take five minutes of your time to explain?"

I planted one foot over the threshold. I wasn't trained as a March of Dimes mother for nothing. He opened the door and I went in. A woman in a housecoat came to a doorway leading off the hall.

"Who is it, Jack?"

"It's a lady who thinks she knows something about our break-in. Mrs—?"

"Caliban."

"Mrs. Caliban, my wife, Georgia."

She looked at me dubiously. She would never have let me in the front door with such a peculiar story, I could tell, but men are such pushovers.

"I only asked for five minutes of your time, Mrs. Stewart, to tell you about a case I'm working on."

"Are you a private investigator?"

"I'm not a licensed one, but I've taken an interest in the Leda Marrs case."

"Leda Marrs. That's the movie star who was killed, right?"

"That's right."

"Are you working with the police?"

"Certainly. Sergeant Fricke and Officer Landau can vouch for me." I hoped she wouldn't ask them to. "I don't believe they were assigned to your case; they work in Homicide. They wouldn't have any reason to suppose that the two cases were connected, but I wonder if you knew that Betty Grumbacher — that's Leda Marrs — once lived in this house with her mother."

That got them. They stared at me, eyes widening. A sudden brush with greatness.

"She did?"

"Yes. And I happen to think that the people who broke into your house were looking for the jewels described in that article." I nodded at the paper, which dangled limply from Mr. Stewart's hand.

They looked at each other, dumbfounded.

"We kept asking the police why they had done so much damage," she said. "They found my jewelry, but they didn't seem satisfied, as if we had heirloom silver hidden in secret compartments under the floorboards or something. Come here, I'll show you."

I followed her into the living room and looked up at the gaping hole in one corner of the ceiling, where she was pointing. The ceiling had been lowered at some point, and the burglars had pushed up a whole section of paneling.

"Now why would an ordinary thief do something like that?" she asked. "We kept asking ourselves, what was it they thought we had?"

"And you think it was that emerald." Mr. Stewart narrowed his eyes thoughtfully.

"That's right. Did you get the impression that they were looking for something small?"

"Yes," she said. "They did a lot of damage here, of course, but they needed to be able to stick their head up in the space between the ceilings. But other places, the damage wasn't nearly that extensive."

I nodded. "It wouldn't take much space to hide an emerald necklace."

"Do you think they found it?" Mr. Stewart asked.

"No. I think they're still looking. In fact, I think they, or perhaps the person who hired them, is hoping the article in the paper will result in the recovery of the necklace."

"How do we know you aren't in cahoots with the men who searched our house?" I liked the way she assumed men had done it. Mr. Stewart, meanwhile, turned pink with embarrassment.

"Well," I said, "you could call Officer Landau in Homicide and ask him to describe me. To tell you the truth, Sergeant Fricke and I don't get along very well, so I'd just as soon you didn't tell him I'd been here." I looked at her when I said this; I knew the final decision would be hers. "He sees me as a meddlesome old lady."

She smiled when I said that.

"The point is I have more at stake in this case than the police do. It happens that Betty Grumbacher was murdered in the apartment upstairs from me, in a building I own. I have kind of a personal grudge against the murderer that the police don't have. They probably would have thought Betty a meddlesome old woman, too, but to me, she's a woman a lot like me, and I hate to think of her murder going unresolved."

"But I thought her son-in-law was arrested."

"Yes, and they have circumstantial evidence against him. He's also charged with assaulting a witness. But he's a wealthy and influential man, and he may walk away from this yet."

"But supposing they find the emerald necklace. Isn't he the heir? Won't it belong to him?"

"Technically, it will belong to his wife. What she'll do with it, I don't know. I guess I really don't want to think about that. What I really want to do, whether Betty's murderer is convicted or not, is to fulfill Betty's wishes. Her will leaves her estate to her daughter. I want to find the contents of that estate."

"Well," she said doubtfully, "it still sounds to me like it will end up in the wrong hands. But if you want to look for it here, I guess it's okay."

Once involved, though, Jack and Georgia were keen on this hunt. You could tell they'd never had anything this exciting happen to them before, and they were dying to turn up the missing jewels under one of their floorboards. Jack even rummaged around and came up with a set of blueprints for the house. We decided to stay together — not because I thought the treasure was booby trapped, or because I thought one of us would run into desperadoes between the second floor and the attic, but because it would be more fun that way. We started in the attic and worked our way down, practically square foot by square foot, until we reached the basement. So far, all we'd found was Jack, Jr.'s prize baseball card, which he'd accused Jimmy Jefferson of lifting when his back was turned, the pin that had held the baby's crib together when she was a baby and before the bed collapsed, and three mismatched barrettes. Jack and Georgia were looking dusty and dispirited, but I had great hopes for the basement.

I rummaged around among the cobwebs, inspected every floor joist, opened every vent or coal chute. Nothing. I felt behind pipes, looked under the water heater, opened the furnace and inspected the shelf on which the filters rested. In one corner was a bin of scrap metal, in another, a bin of scrap wood. I rummaged some more, and came up with my only find of the day: a rectangular piece of rough wood about eighteen inches by eight inches. Along one side was a row of bent nails, with bits of excelsior still hanging on. It appeared to be part of a crate and still showed an address label intact: Miss Betty Grumbacher. The stamps were inscribed in Arabic, and the date on the postmark was March 14, 1943. It proved to be the only identifiable trace we discovered of the Grumbachers' presence in the house.

Jack and Georgia were crushed, but they promised to keep looking. I don't know where they thought they were going to look, but Georgia was gazing thoughtfully at the back yard when she said it. I tried to sound definite in my opinion that the emeralds weren't here. I didn't want it on my head if they dismantled the swing set, rented a backhoe, and dug their way to China with nothing to show for it.

The thing was I had begun to get an idea what we were looking for. But I didn't see where Betty could have hidden it.

When I got home, I found scattered on the floor yesterday's mail, which I'd dumped on a table by the front door until I was sufficiently strong or inebriated enough to confront the bills. My loyal housemates had done their best to obliterate my accounts payable by shredding the bills into confetti. I picked up a piece of one. *Goddamn*, I said to myself and anybody else who was listening, Stormwater Management. I already paid a damn sewer bill. Who gave these schmoes the right to collect another thirty bucks off me? Especially since every time it rained I had to wear hip waders to keep my socks dry and wear water wings in my basement. As far as I could see, the city's storm water management policy ran to laissez-faire, a term I learned when Franny was an econ major at Purdue.

That was when inspiration hit. I went to the telephone and called Walter Smith, hoping that he didn't spend his Sundays in church.

"Walter," I said, when he answered the phone and I'd identified myself, "I was wondering what it is that you did in the city engineer's office." I didn't mention that I'd been zoning out the first time he told me about his place of employment, since it hadn't interested me at all.

"Oh, well, the city engineer, you know, he's in charge of the city's infrastructure — bridges, streets, hillside supports, stuff like that. We worked with other city departments, of course, but anything that had to do with the infrastructure we had a hand in."

"How about sewers and storm drains?" .

"Yes, well, we worked with the water department on that and of course, storm water management. But we had to approve any plans for new lines, you know."

"So did you actually go down in the sewers? I mean, are there tunnels under the city for sewer maintenance?" In my mind's eye I was seeing a climax out of *The Third Man*.

"Well, there's some," he conceded.

"Big enough to hide something in? Something fairly bulky, I mean."

"Oh, no, not like that. But what kind of thing was you thinking about? Couldn't be too big, you know. Well, not if you wanted to hide it, you see."

"Aren't there any abandoned lines? You know . . . tunnels that aren't used anymore, but ones that might still be accessible?"

"No, nothing like that." He paused. "Not like the subway tunnels."

The subway tunnels! Here I'd lived in Cincinnati more than half my life and you'd think I'd just arrived on the bus from Tuscaloosa. Everybody knows about the subway tunnels in Cincinnati. It was back in the twenties the city started building a subway, dug the damn tunnels and everything, and then gave up on the project. See, after all that time and money, it suddenly dawned on somebody that they were going to all this trouble to get people from downtown to Northside, and who the hell wanted to go to Northside? Even then it was suffering an image problem. You could still see the station entrances off I-75. Wasn't more than six months since I'd heard a story on the local news about trying to get filmmakers interested in the tunnels as an ideal location for shooting subterranean scenes.

Lucky there was carpet on the floor I was pounding my head on. Sadie sat three feet away and regarded me with a quizzical air.

"The city engineer's office was in charge of maintaining those tunnels? I mean the subway tunnels, right?"

"Well, sure, you could say that. Not that there was much maintaining to do since nobody used them. Mostly we just inspected them once a year for structural damage that could affect the ground over them."

"How do you get into them?"

"Why, you can't get into them now, unless you have a key to the padlocks. They're sealed, but they have these iron doors with padlocks."

"And you had a key?"

"Sometimes I had one, if I was assigned to inspect them. You know, it's kind of funny you should bring all this up. Betty, she was interested in them tunnels."

"Was she? Did you ever take her into one?"

"Why, yes, I did. It was after we was separated, I don't recollect just when. We talked from time to time, you know, and she got this bee in her bonnet about them tunnels, and nothing would do but what she had to have me take her through one."

"I don't suppose you ever missed a key to one of the padlocks?"

"Why, I did, too! How did you know? I believe, come to think of it, it was right after that time I took her down there, because I called up and asked her if she saw me put it back in my pocket. She couldn't remember. But I'd locked the lock when I left, I knew that much, so I thought, well, you've gone and dropped it somewhere. I didn't think anybody would know what it was if they found it, so I didn't think anything more about it."

"Mr. Smith," I said, "I suddenly find that I also have an overwhelming desire to see one of those subway tunnels. Do you think you could arrange it?"

CHAPTER 27

It was pouring down rain — my retribution for speaking ill of the Stormwater Management folks. The water came streaming down the incline to our left, off Central Parkway, and formed a river at our feet. To our right, the traffic on I-75 threw up a cloud of mud. If our spirits were undampened, our bodies were soaked.

Al got the worst of it since she had taken off from work and was wearing hose and pumps. Kevin and Mel were in jeans, I was in a skirt and Adidas, which I felt sure would disintegrate and drop off my feet at any moment. Walter had been wearing a suit, but I'd persuaded him to leave the jacket in the car. Landau was in his shirtsleeves, playing hooky from sitting around and shooting the bull at Daily Donuts. Fricke had shown no interest in coming. One of Walter's successors, a young Black man named James from the city engineer's office, was fitting the key in the padlock. From James's expression, you could tell he thought we were all crazy. Probably right. We looked like the goddamn survivors from *Journey to the Center of the Earth*, and we hadn't even gone anywhere yet. So far, I'd only asked to see the tunnel entrance closest to downtown — the one Walter had lost the key to. Wait till I asked to see the rest.

James gave the heavy iron door a yank and it slid sideways with a loud metallic clank. He shone a powerful flashlight over the dim cavern within.

"Watch your step," he said. "I guess Walter already told you about the ghost." Everybody's a comedian.

We stepped in.

Kevin sneezed. Mold allergies. I'd especially wanted Kevin along, mold or no mold, but I hadn't told him why.

We walked a few dozen yards to where the tunnel opened up on both sides. We were standing in the area once intended for a platform, facing a set of tracks that had never materialized.

I shivered. "I hope it's cold enough," I muttered to myself. James looked at me like I'd wished for an earthquake.

"You go that way," I said to Kevin, who was holding another flashlight, "and I'll go this way."

"You mean," he said, in a mock-horrified voice, "we're going to *split up*?"

"Drop bread crumbs," I said. "And if you see any rats, send them in the other direction."

"I still don't know what you expect to find, Mrs. Caliban," James sighed. "These tunnels are inspected once a year. If there was anything hidden down here, we'd find it."

I hated to admit he was right, so I didn't say anything. We headed south, toward the city.

We'd walked for less than five minutes, when I spotted a recess where boxes had been piled.

"What's that?" We went closer.

"Stuff left behind by the builders, looks like."

The boxes were stamped with the name of a construction firm. On top of the pile in front were three boxes filled with tile.

"Waste of the taxpayers' money," Al grumbled. "Didn't even use the damn tile on another project."

"Maybe it's special subway tile," Mel said.

I was lifting the top box, but James took it away from me. "I'll do that, Mrs. Caliban. What you want to move this stuff for, anyway?"

The next box down was empty. When I moved it, I spotted another pile behind this one, covered with an old tarp which smelled of mildew. I felt little spiders do a tarantella on the back of my neck. I reached over and pulled off the tarp.

It was pretty goddamned dramatic, if I do say so myself, even if my Adidas did squish when I bent over.

"There," I said. *"That's* what I'm looking for. Somebody call Kevin."

As we moved the first pile of boxes aside, another pile emerged behind it — a neat pile of wooden crates stacked lengthwise, more than thirty of them. I stood and admired Betty's handiwork.

"What is it?" somebody asked.

I pulled out a screwdriver and pried up the lid on the first crate. It moved easily. The cover was intended to hide the contents from view, not to protect them from damage. I extracted a slip of paper. It was a Shakespearean love sonnet — the one about the fallen leaves and old age — handwritten in ink on yellowed paper headed by some kind of seal. I reached in the crate again and pulled out a bottle. I passed it to Kevin. In the dim light of the tunnel, I saw his eyebrows hit his hairline.

"Not bad. A 1928 Chateau Magdelaine."

"Not bad, my ass!" James was looking over his shoulder. "Do you know how much that's worth?" James was demonstrating unexpected areas of expertise that made me glad he'd come along. "Let me see that." He studied the label a minute, then brought out a penknife and started attacking the nearest crate. Meanwhile, I'd liberated another bottle.

"Chateau Petrus, 1919. Do you think all the bottles are likely to be this good?"

"Phyl said the sheik never shopped bargain basements."

"There's a note in this one, too: 'All my love, forever.' Romantic son-of-a-gun, wasn't he?"

"There's a fortune here!" James exclaimed. Walter Smith was looking perturbed.

"It's okay, Walt," I said. "Remember, you said even Jesus drank wine. Just think how happy this cellar would have made him."

"Are you saying somebody sent her all these bottles?" James asked. I nodded. "Well, he must not have known she wasn't drinking it. Look — a Sauterne. Chateau d'Yquem. We'll be lucky if it hasn't gone bad."

"I don't even know whether they corresponded. This may have been the only form of communication between them." I was studying the top of one of the crates under a flashlight. The postmark was March 14, 1936. "From the numbers and the dates, I suspect he sent her one a year, to mark some kind of anniversary. Her birthday wasn't in March."

"But it was about the middle of March when we separated!" Walter burst out, intrigued in spite of himself. "You know — that time I came home and found her — and she had gotten something in the mail that day, too! Remember, I told you."

"Yeah, I guess she got one of the sheik's annual love letters."

"I thought we were looking for emeralds," Mel said.

James was clucking to himself over his latest discovery.

"We are. Keep looking."

There was a sharp intake of breath from Kevin. He was staring at the bottle in his hands.

"What is it?"

I had never seen Kevin struck speechless. I took the bottle away from him and handed it to James.

"Chateau Lafite. 1806." His voice was a reverent whisper. "It can't be."

"Why not?"

"It must be very rare. Extremely rare. A Chateau Lafite from the early nineteenth century?"

Kevin spoke. "More than that. Until this one, there were only two bottles known to be in existence."

"How do you know that?" Mel said.

Kevin shrugged. "I'm a fountain of useless knowledge."

"How much is something like that worth?" Al asked, before I could get a word in edgewise. "More than a thousand?"

"Probably more than twenty times that. I don't know,"

Mel was thumping a crate on the bottom and shaking it. James lunged to catch whatever dropped out and came up with something that glimmered green in the dim light. At first, just for a moment, I thought a bottle of wine had broken in the crate.

"Eureka!" Mel said triumphantly. "The Velazquez emerald! Stuffed in the bottom of the crate with all this paper. Looks like — love letters."

The women crowded around. The men glanced at the rock, then went back to opening crates. Except for Walter, who ended up holding the emeralds.

"'My darling,'" Al read aloud, "'since I couldn't be there this morning to awaken you with kisses, I send these emissaries to awaken you with their sweat scent—'"

"That's 'sweet,' not 'sweat.' Sweet scent."

"—'sweet scent, and remind you of the sweatness — the sweetness — of our passion, which, unlike these lovely flowers, will never fade.'"

"Is this guy for real?" Mel asked. "Holy Toledo! It sounds like a scene out of an old movie."

"That's probably where he learned it," I said. "They didn't teach him that at Cambridge, or wherever he was educated."

The boys were oohing and ahhing over a bottle with a funny-looking label.

"Château Mouton Rothschild, 1958. Label by Salvador Dali."

"'We have not time, but eternity to gather.'" James was reading from a note out of one of the crates. "Oh, wait, maybe it's 'together.'"

"'Here's looking at you, kid'? That must have been in — yep, it was. 1943. *Casablanca.*"

"An eclectic writer of love letters. I like that," I said.

When we had finished, we had examined thirty-four bottles of wine and replaced them in their crates. I figured at least three more were already accounted for — two bottles of champagne, and something else worth a thousand dollars.

"So, I don't get it," Mel said. "If they loved each other so much, why didn't they get married?"

Kevin gave her a withering look. "Sheiks didn't marry American girls."

"What's-his-face, the one who married Rita Hayworth, did."

"That was years later, after the war. Anyway, maybe our sheik came from a more traditional family. He probably married the girl his parents picked out for him."

"So he married a suitable match and every year on their anniversary he sent Betty a bottle of wine. Hard to imagine. Don't you think they ever met afterward?"

"Who knows? But I doubt it. I'll bet it was the way Phyl Stinger said — he was in love with some goddamn romantic idea. Anybody who can write that kind of stuff, year in and year out, must be. If he'd seen Betty years afterward, it might have destroyed his illusion."

"But did he know he had a daughter?"

"I don't know. Maybe we'll find out when we read all the letters and notes."

"But Mrs. Caliban," Walter put in, "I don't understand how she managed all this." He gestured with his cane at the pile before us. "I see now that Betty took my key, but how did she get it all down here? And when?"

"I don't know that, either. I mean, to get it down here, she might have brought it bottle by bottle, crate by crate. Or she might have had help from a friend."

"And she even stuffed newspaper and cardboard in the bottom to tilt the bottles forward, so that the corks wouldn't dry out," James said in awe.

"So this was Betty's estate, the legacy she left her daughter. But how could anybody find it?"

"I imagine Lucille knew about it. But she may have been the only one."

"Okay, more to the point," said Kevin, "how did *you* find it? You knew what we were looking for and you knew where it was. How?"

"From the clues Betty left in her safe deposit box. The articles, remember? One was about her first movie, *The Beautiful Martyr*, and the words 'Roman set' were underlined. What had impressed the pants off the reviewer was the set for the Roman catacombs. In another article, the word 'wine' was underlined."

"So were other words, as I recall."

"Yeah, it was pretty hard to tell, after all those years. And there was something about 'queen,' so maybe she wanted us to know that whatever she had was located somewhere in Cincinnati, the Queen City, or maybe her hand slipped. But when I saw the piece of wood from the crate in the basement of Betty's house and the excelsior, I got to thinking. It had to be something that fit in a crate that size. And I suddenly remembered the champagne somebody — presumably Betty — had sent to her daughter on two special occasions. There must be more champagne here, right?"

"Yeah, a few bottles. Probably flat."

"Right. And somebody told Helen it was expensive champagne. So I began to think of something besides the emerald."

"Do you really think she knew this wine was worth a lot of money?"

"She probably knew the sheik's taste, and maybe he'd taught her something about vintage wines, or maybe she'd picked it up elsewhere."

"But she didn't know enough to know that you shouldn't keep white wines this long. Unless she just had incredible faith that they would turn out okay."

"I can't believe this lady owned all this great wine and never drank a drop of it." James shook his head. "Especially since she was out on the street and everything."

“She viewed it as her daughter’s legacy,” I said. “She wouldn’t touch it. The real kicker, as far as I’m concerned, is that everybody and his parakeet seems to have thought that she’d drunk up her goddamn fortune.”

CHAPTER 28

I was hosing down the kitty litter boxes out in the front yard when a white BMW slid up to the curb. Four of the biggest guys I ever saw unfolded themselves on either side and stood regarding the Catatonia Arms. They were all wearing suits and shades and looked like walking advertisements for Nautilus. One of them had his hand inside his coat and I hoped he wasn't packing. All I had was a garden hose.

"Mrs. Caliban?"

"Yes?" To tell you the truth, I was caught off guard, or I might have denied it.

"I'm Raymond Jakes, Leon's brother. These my brothers — Alex, Charles, and Junior."

"Pleased to meet you." I shook hands all around, and wondered what penalty they could impose for child endangerment. I still had the hose in my left hand, spewing water all over my new Adidas. Suave, that's me.

"Pleasure's ours," Junior said, and flashed me a smile.

"We come to thank you for all you done for Leon," Raymond said gravely.

"All I did?" I said cautiously. "I didn't do anything."

"Yes, ma'am, you surely did. We *know* Leon didn't catch no big-time criminal all by his own self."

"Well—"

"Leon's a hero," said Alex. "He love it. Mayor shake his hand, police give him a special citation to hang on his wall, reporters come to ask him was it like this or like that, everybody look at him like he important."

"Leon ain't never had a chance to be important before," added Charles. "Ain't never been no whiz kid, I expect you know that. Always been the slow one in the family. He depend on my mother to tell him he special. She say God got a special mission for him in life. Now he begin to believe it."

"That's what we come to thank you for."

"Are you kidding?" I finally dropped the damn hose. Junior jumped and just missed ruining his Italian leather shoes. "Leon *is* a hero. Why, we would probably both have been shot if it hadn't been for Leon. Hell, the cops wouldn't hardly have a case against Prescott if it weren't for Leon. I said all along, Leon was my ace in the hole, and he was, too. I counted on Leon, and he came through. There's nothing to thank me for."

"Well, hadn't been for you, he would never been involved. It mean a lot to him that you had confidence in him."

"I thought," I rejoined feebly, "maybe you were pissed off because of the danger he was in, may still be in."

Alex waved this aside. "We can take care of Leon. Woulda took care of him then, but we were out of town."

"Just as well, turns out," said Charles. "This be something Leon did on his own, without his brothers around. He real proud of that."

"So we wanted to express our appreciation, and to tell you if it's anything we can do for you any time, just let us know. Anything at all."

"We got a lot of friends." Junior smiled benignantly again. "And business connections. Maybe we can help you out sometime."

"Thanks, I appreciate it. Like I say, I'm glad things turned out so well for Leon."

"Anything we can do," Alex echoed.

"I don't think there's anything, thanks, unless you can get me a P.I. license without my two years of experience." I was kidding, of course.

Raymond looked thoughtful. "Charles?"

Charles had been momentarily distracted by Sidney, who had bolted out of the bushes to attack his shoelaces. He grinned, scooped Sidney up with one hand, and cradled his attacker, belly up, in his arms, tickling a healthy expanse of furry tummy.

"Hey, there, little buddy," he said. "You better start working out with us."

"Charles," Raymond repeated patiently.

"We can look into that, sure."

"Okay," said Raymond. "We see what we can do. We call you in a few days. Leon got the number."

I felt a little faint when they shook my hand again, got in the car, and drove off. It was a hot day. I had probably been hallucinating.

* * *

Saturday afternoon at about the same time, I answered the door and found Fred's old pal Herb Munch standing there. Sidney wasn't on guard duty, apparently, so he must have been watching Felix cartoons in air-conditioned splendor at Kevin's.

"Haven't heard from you lately, Catherine." That Herb. Nimble-tongued and quick-witted as Daffy Duck.

"No."

"Thought I should check in and see how you're doing."

"Oh. I'm fine."

"What you been doing with yourself? I figured you'd be off on a cruise by now."

"Really? Why would you figure that?"

"Oh, well, you know. Moving out of the old neighborhood, getting this place." He surveyed the room with a sour look. "Cutting the old ties. I figured you'd be — you know, bored. Lonely."

I stared at him. Bored? Lonely? *Me?* If anything, my life was overcrowded and overwhelmingly eventful. He didn't know this, of course, because I'd kept a low profile in the papers and given Leon all the glory.

Herb had settled himself in a living room chair.

The door flew open and Al stomped in wearing a new dress, pinned crooked at the hem, dangling price tags from the sleeves.

"Kevin says it's too short. What do *you* think?"

Kevin followed her in, trailing a tape measure. Sidney was perched on his shoulder.

"I keep trying to tell her, Mrs. C. They're wearing them longer this season."

"Not *that* long. Kevin, I'm a short person. I can't wear a skirt down to my ankles."

Sidney was beginning to eye Herb's ankles.

There was a loud thud on the ceiling. Mel had dropped a barbell.

Kevin was studying Herb with apparent alarm, as if contemplating launching into his routine for prospective tenants he considered unsuitable. I had a feeling he'd already run a few off when I wasn't around to supervise.

Sophie raced through the living room with Sadie at her heels.

The washing machine began to dance heavily across the basement floor.

The phone rang.

A husky young woman in painter's pants stuck her head in the door.

"Hi. Mel Carter live here?"

"Upstairs," I said.

In the background, my new answering machine started up after the second ring. "This is 555-5443. I can't answer right now, but if you'll leave a message at the beep—"

Holly Near began to sing loudly upstairs. I hoped Herb couldn't hear the lyrics. If he heard them, I hoped he couldn't understand them, which was probably the case.

Another head popped in. "Mel?"

"Upstairs," we said in unison.

"Mel's feminist reading group," Al explained.

I could hear Mabel talking to the answering machine, while her lovebirds chirped in the background. "Cat? Are you there? If you're there, pick up the damn phone."

Sophie strolled through and laid a dead mouse at Herb's feet.

"Maybe I'd better get going," he said.

"Maybe you'd better," I said. Then, "Thanks for stopping in," as an afterthought.

"Let me know if you—"

He bumped into a towering woman with short gray hair and an earring in one nostril.

"Sorry," he mumbled. "Mel's upstairs."

Kevin and Al exited, still squabbling. Sidney had decided to escort Herb off the premises.

I heard Mel's voice boom, "Go ahead and start without me. I gotta borrow Kevin's microwave for the brownies."

I had just pitched the mouse out the back door when the goddamn doorbell rang again.

"Look," I said, wrenching the door open.

Standing before me was a Black man of about my age dressed in slacks and a sports coat. Average height, neatly trimmed mustache and sideburns, a little on the paunchy side.

"I came to see about the apartment."

He could have been a Martian asking directions to Jupiter. I wasn't thinking.

"The apartment?" I frowned.

"Don't you have an apartment to rent? The sign says you do."

"Oh. The apartment."

"I suppose it's a one-bedroom."

"Uh, yes."

"May I see it?"

"See it?"

"The apartment."

"We haven't quite finished cleaning it yet." Well, I knew there weren't any visible bloodstains, and the smell was gone, thank God, but I hadn't gotten around to replacing the carpet yet.

"That's okay. I don't mind."

"I, uh, actually, I haven't been in there in a while. I don't know what it's like."

"I don't mind."

"Have you been looking at other apartments?" None of my goddamn business, actually, but I was trying to decide whether to tell this nice-looking gentleman that the last resident had been a corpse.

"No. I came here first. I like the street, and my daughter lives over on Cherry."

"Oh."

"Is there some reason you don't want to show me this apartment, ma'am?" His tone was even, his voice was quiet, but there was something in his eyes. Suddenly, I realized what he thought.

"Oh, no. That is, yes, I guess so. The truth is, Mr.—"

"Fogg. Moses Fogg."

"The truth is, Mr. Fogg, somebody died there quite recently."

"You'd be surprised how many apartments in Cincinnati that could be said about."

"Yes, well, she didn't die, exactly, though. I mean, she was murdered."

He looked at me calmly. "You'd be surprised how many apartments in Cincinnati *that* could be said about," he replied mildly. "I ought to know. I'm a retired police officer."

"Oh!" I exclaimed, no doubt crowning his impression of me as a complete nincompoop. "You don't mind, then?"

"Open her up," he said, smiling a little. "I like it, I take it. If the rent's reasonable."

"How would you feel about one-fifty?" I mentally subtracted thirty dollars in case there were any lingering bloodstains.

"Sounds okay to me. Let's see it."

I rummaged in the desk drawer and brought out the key. He followed me up and looked the place over.

"I guess this was the Grumbacher murder. I hope he gets what's coming to him, that doctor, but you can't ever tell. He might get off yet, or plea bargain himself down to a misdemeanor. Well, Mrs. Caliban, it looks okay to me. There's just one thing, though. I got a dog."

"A dog?" I echoed.

"She's just a little old thing, a little beagle pup my daughter gave me because she thought I was lonely after my wife passed last year."

"How does she feel about cats?"

He chuckled. "She worships the ground they walk on."

"An admirable attitude. Okay, she's in. What's her name?"

"Winnie." He looked sheepish. "We named her after Winnie Mandela, the South African leader."

By now, we were in the hall outside Kevin's door and he appeared magically. Kevin has a sixth sense for events in which his interest is involved.

"Kevin, this is Mr. Fogg. He wants to take the apartment upstairs."

"Wonderful!" Kevin exclaimed. "Why don't I take him in and introduce him around while you get the lease?"

I wasn't fooled for a minute. If Mr. Fogg didn't pass muster he'd have no interest in my lease when I got back. Still, it was just as well for him to know what he was getting himself into, so I took my time about the lease.

When I entered Kevin's living room, I was alarmed to hear Kevin's voice raised in anger. Oh, shit, I thought: a scene. I was torn between rescue and retreat. I tiptoed into the dining room. Through the kitchen door I could see Kevin standing with his hands on his hips, glaring at somebody I couldn't see. I froze.

Then, Kevin broke his pose, and a wave of laughter struck my ears. Kevin had been telling one of his stories. At the doorway I stopped and surveyed the scene in the kitchen, the lease in my hand.

Kevin was grinning ear to ear and stirring a pot on the stove under the watchful eye of Sophie, who was perched on the refrigerator. The other three sat around the table. Moses Fogg sat on one side with Sadie curled up on his lap and Sidney wrapped around his ankles. His head was thrown back and his palms were flat on his knees. He was shaking with laughter. So was Mel, who sat bolt upright while her shoulders rose and fell. Al had a hand on one of Mel's shoulders, as if to steady herself. She was alternately snorting and gasping with mirth.

For a moment I stood looking at them. My gang. Lonely and bored? At my time of life? Never.

"What's so funny?" I said.

THE END

THE JOFFE BOOKS STORY

We began in 2014 when Jasper agreed to publish his mum's much-rejected romance novel and it became a bestseller.

Since then we've grown into the largest independent publisher in the UK. We're extremely proud to publish some of the very best writers in the world, including Joy Ellis, Faith Martin, Caro Ramsay, Helen Forrester, Simon Brett and Robert Goddard. Everyone at Joffe Books loves reading and we never forget that it all begins with the magic of an author telling a story.

We are proud to publish talented first-time authors, as well as established writers whose books we love introducing to a new generation of readers.

We won Trade Publisher of the Year at the Independent Publishing Awards in 2023 and Best Publisher Award in 2024 at the People's Book Prize. We have been shortlisted for Independent Publisher of the Year at the British Book Awards for the last five years, and were shortlisted for the Diversity and Inclusivity Award at the 2022 Independent Publishing Awards. In 2023 we were shortlisted for Publisher of the Year at the RNA Industry Awards, and in 2024 we were shortlisted at the CWA Daggers for the Best Crime and Mystery Publisher.

We built this company with your help, and we love to hear from you, so please email us about absolutely anything bookish at feedback@joffebooks.com.

If you want to receive free books every Friday and hear about all our new releases, join our mailing list here: www.joffebooks.com/freebooks.

And when you tell your friends about us, just remember: it's pronounced Joffe as in coffee or toffee!

Printed in Dunstable, United Kingdom

79023480R00129